"Help!" Gilly cried

Then a man appeared. He was tall and wide shouldered, swathed in a long black coat. His collar was raised and his features were concealed behind a dark scarf. A black fedora was pulled down low over his forehead. He was very dashing. Very Humphrey Bogart. Just under the hat brim, Gilly caught the reflection of sunglasses. He was wearing sunglasses? At night? In the deepest shadows of a dark alley?

"Who are you?" she whispered as her savior swept down on the thugs who'd been chasing her and vanquished them. Then the man came close, and whispered, "You'd be advised to stay off the streets."

Movement farther down the alley caught Gilly's attention—but only for a heartbeat. Then Gilly turned back to the mystery man.

Gone. He had been Gilly's dream man—and now he was gone!

Dear Reader,

You're about to meet one of the most mysterious, magical men!

Lucas Blackthorn is many things, but none of them is ordinary, as Gilly Quinn—and you—are about to find out.

And neither are any of the heroes in American Romance's ongoing series MORE THAN MEN. Whether their extraordinary powers enable them to grant you three wishes or live forever, their greatest power is that of seduction.

We're delighted at your enthusiastic response to the MORE THAN MEN stories, and happy we can bring you more of what you want to read.

So turn the page—and be seduced by Lucas Blackthorn. It's an experience you'll never forget!

Regards,

Debra Matteucci
Senior Editor & Editorial Coordinator
Harlequin Books
300 East 42nd Street
New York, NY 10017

JULIE
KISTLER

TOUCH ME NOT

Harlequin Books

TORONTO • NEW YORK • LONDON
AMSTERDAM • PARIS • SYDNEY • HAMBURG
STOCKHOLM • ATHENS • TOKYO • MILAN
MADRID • WARSAW • BUDAPEST • AUCKLAND

ISBN 0-373-16690-7

TOUCH ME NOT

Copyright © 1997 by Julie Kistler.

This edition published by arrangement with Harlequin Books S.A.

® and TM are trademarks of the publisher. Trademarks indicated with ® are registered in the United States Patent and Trademark Office, the Canadian Trade Marks Office and in other countries.

Printed in U.S.A.

Prologue

Lucas Blackthorn was not amused.

"Hey, guy, take my picture!" A freckled kid with flaming red hair ran right in front of Luke's battered old Leica, waving his arms and offering a wide gap-toothed grin. A perfect duplicate of Opie, just like the one on old black-and-white TV. "Come on, take me!"

Luke just shook his head. Under other circumstances it might've made an okay photo, another Lucas Blackthorn original to add to the portfolio. Light and dark, sunshine and shadows... Contrast. That was what always caught his eye, whether he was shooting a farmer and his cow or a bomb bursting in air.

The boy's Technicolor all-American looks set against the exotic setting of ancient ruins, the blazing afternoon sun adding shadows to his freckles, even the expression on the nanny's face behind him as she tried to grab the kid and get him back behind the barrier— it might've made a fine picture, if Luke weren't so damn bored with the whole scene.

Lucas Blackthorn, reduced to Norman Rockwell photo opportunities.

Fresh from a teary memorial service in rainy, grainy Berlin, he'd been sent to shoot the mass graves of a war-crimes scene in Eastern Europe. Chilling. Riveting. Drama every time he looked through the lens. His black-and-white photos of sorrow and despair had rocketed around the world, courtesy of IPB, the International Press Bureau, which paid his bills and set his assignments. The words "Pulitzer prize" were on his boss's lips constantly these days.

"So where do you go after that?" he muttered aloud. "Disney World?"

Not Disney World, of course. Just a sun-drenched Mediterranean island celebrating the discovery of some new cave paintings. A lazy indolent place with the crumbling relics of an ancient palace and some kind of major find underneath it. Exciting to some folks. Very historic, he was sure. But not his cup of tea. Not in a million years.

Okay, so the scholars were excited, and the government of Crete was treating it like God's gift to tourism.

But to Lucas Blackthorn, who'd earned his place in the pantheon of photojournalists in the world's hottest and coldest spots, it was deadly dull. R and R, his editor said. Sunny Crete. You'll love it. You deserve it.

Well, it was sunny all right. White heat, turquoise water, the colors so bright they hurt his eyes. Fawning dignitaries, nervous scientist types, everybody hovering and pestering him and driving him crazy.

He could camp out in a dirty, cold hotel room for days on end, existing on saltines and a couple of beers, in search of truth on the other side of his lens. But sunbathing, gazing at crystal waters, eating fancy meals, waiting for a five-minute appointment with a prehistoric finger painting—it was making him nuts.

He hadn't even been in the cave in question yet.

He'd tried to sneak in to get an idea of the lighting, work on an angle, maybe snap a few pictures in cool solitude before everybody else tramped by and churned up dust. But the official types were holding everyone back to heighten the suspense. Not even Lucas Blackthorn, award-winning photographer from IPB, the guy who knew more angles than a geometry teacher, could get past the guard and the barriers.

"It's fragile," they explained in hushed tones. "The cave has not been completely excavated yet. We must do this carefully."

Luke frowned as he peered through his lens, checking out the faces in the crowd. What a sideshow. Treating some prehistoric artwork as if it were life and death. Well, he'd seen life and death. And this wasn't it.

Finally a smiling man with a big black mustache and a bright white suit indicated it was time to line up to go into the cave for the big unveiling. "One at a time please," he said in careful English.

Other photographers jockeyed to get in first, but Luke ambled into line near the end. He didn't care. Any cave paintings that had been there since King Minos ruled Crete would last until he got his turn.

The redheaded kid zoomed in behind him, his nanny nowhere in sight. Guess ol' Opie had ditched his chaperon. "Hey, you sure you don't wanna take my picture?" he asked happily. He couldn't seem to stand still, darting around like a puppy on adoption day at the pound. "I play soccer and I'm real limber and I can kick myself in the head. Wanna see?"

"Yeah, sure." Luke even managed a smile. That red hair was pretty striking. Reminded him of an old friend who'd had just as much of a tendency to bounce around like a jumping bean. Her hair wasn't quite as fire-engine red as this kid's. But red enough to be a reminder.

Gilly. He never had been able to say no to Gilly.

Dutifully, Luke snapped a few pictures of the kid, which he already knew wouldn't be keepers. Turned out Opie really could kick himself in the head, but the pictures weren't going to be all that great. When Luke's heart and mind weren't engaged in the work, his photos suffered.

"So," he said, moving around to the other side of his subject, pulling a fish-eye lens out of his pocket, looking for a different angle that would make the picture seem fresher. "What are you doing here? This seems like an old crowd for you. What are you—world's youngest art historian?"

"Nah," the boy said, taking the question perfectly seriously. "My dad's, like, the undersecretary of something and I'm here to get my picture taken with him later. It's one of those family-values things."

Cynical to the ways of the world. And at such a young age.

"So, you interested in this cave painting at all?" Luke inquired, as the line inched ahead.

"Maybe. I think it's animals. My dad said bulls. Like Chicago and Michael Jordan, y'know. Bulls are cool."

Lucas smiled wider. "Yeah, bulls are cool." They'd reached the entrance to the cave now, Luke's small pal still bouncing around with energy while uniformed men with rifles policed the line.

Luke offered a mock salute to the guards as he passed, but they paid him no attention. Inside it was immediately darker, cooler and fairly narrow, with a steep downward incline. So far there was nothing to see but reddish cloudy dirt, underfoot and all around. A network of two-by-fours were braced against the walls. Didn't look too sturdy. Luke reached out and grabbed Opie, who was tugging one of the support beams. "Not a good idea," Luke said dryly.

"Yeah, but look!" Opie eagerly pointed to a smaller corridor—just his size—meandering away from the main branch but blocked by the beam. There were several such corridors, all radiating from the main passageway. "Wonder where all these little tunnels go, huh?"

"No place good, that's for sure," Luke said with a laugh.

Already those in the front of the line were winding toward the entrance, looping back in a one-way circle. Luke heard "most impressive" and "spectacular" bandied about, but some people would say that about anything, so he took it with a grain of salt. Still, he felt the faint stirrings of hope that maybe there would be something to photograph here, after all. Was that excitement in the air? Or just claustrophobia?

The line moved forward, still painfully slow. Opie was clearly getting bored and he started jumping up and down to keep himself occupied. That wouldn't have bothered Luke, except for the close quarters in this dim corridor. Still, he and his camera bags had ventured into places a lot more dangerous than this.

"Hope the light gets better," he grumbled, casting a jaded eye at the shadowy cave walls. He liked shadows as much as the next guy, but he wasn't sure he'd be able to get the kind of detailed shots he wanted. He hadn't been allowed to scope out the paintings early on or set up any lighting, and he feared the worst.

But suddenly things became much brighter. The group emerged from the long, narrow passage into a wide round room lit with freestanding spotlights. Luke noticed smaller passages threading out of the cavern. He craned his neck, managing to get a glimpse of the shadowy paintings splashed against the wall.

He sucked in his breath. Impressive indeed. There were some smaller, fainter drawings of something— birds maybe—a couple of deep red handprints off to one side and then the centerpiece. Powerful and proud, broad across the chest, the massive bull had so much life and fire you could almost hear the air snorting from its flared nostrils.

Luke stepped back, almost tripping over Opie. "Sorry," he said automatically. He put out a hand to steady the kid, but he didn't take his eyes off the animal on the wall across the way.

He wasn't normally given to flights of fancy. Picasso, Monet, da Vinci—it didn't matter what style of fine art you stuck in front of him, he could appreciate the technique or the approach, but on a fundamental level, it just didn't reach him.

But this did.

Stick figures, really, no more, done up in slashing strokes of earth brown and clay red, flowing across the cave wall as if some prehistoric genius had poured his soul straight onto the wall.

"Magnificent," Luke whispered. Without thinking, he reached for his Leica, already calculating the light and the exposure. The noise, the crowd, even Opie pushing from behind, eager to see for himself around the taller grown-ups, didn't faze him. Luke kept clicking, changing angles, changing lenses, never wavering from his focus on the bull on the wall.

Finally Luke was dead center in front of the paintings. He had the oddest sensation, as if the bull itself were roaring in his ears. It wasn't so much a sound as a vibration, and the air around him felt heavy, dense, thick with meaning. *Portent of doom,* he thought, but had no idea why.

"Can you feel that?" he asked quickly, but he got only blank faces in response as the people around him shuffled restlessly, waiting their turn.

He shook his head. But the eerie feeling persisted.

It was the strangest thing, but he couldn't take his eyes off the wall, where the mighty bull, painted there so long ago, charged in front of him. Wordlessly, nervelessly, he kept lining up shots, until he felt breathless and dizzy.

"Hey, cool, huh?" Opie shouted, bending his eager little face right in front of the lens. "Want to take my picture with the bull?"

"Uh, no," Luke started to say, but the roaring noise suddenly became much louder, with an underlying vibration that sent fear to the pit of his stomach. Why? What was that noise?

Now the others seemed to pick up on it; heads turned this way and that, and one person let out a little yelp. Then one of the spotlights trembled and swayed, casting tipsy circles of light against the walls. They all stared, riveted, watching the light pitch to the side, shattering glass as it fell to the packed earth. In a cacophony of different languages, people began to demand answers. And then the other light pole toppled, too.

"Run! Get out of here!" someone shouted. Panic seemed to rise like a cloud of smoke. "The cave is crumbling!"

Jostling, shoving, stumbling, they all turned back and ran for the narrow passageway as fast as they could. But Luke was the farthest from the exit, and he knew he'd never get through that crowd. He judged the situation, quickly decided to stay where he was, waiting for the stampede to subside.

One two-by-four and then another fell headlong into the crowd. People were screaming and crying as dirt and support beams tumbled from the walls, nipping at their heels.

Luke stood still, listening, still shooting pictures in the dim light. There was drama now, life and death, and he knew even without thinking that he was getting great stuff. As he kept clicking, he watched the herd of folks scramble to safety, saw that Opie had stumbled to his knees, took in the swelling rumble of earth and ancient stone, as the whole support system of wood beams threatened to cave in.

The kid was in trouble. Luke's hand stilled. Time to move. Now or never.

The dirt was piling up, blocking the exit, and Luke had to leap over falling timbers and heaps of loose soil to get to the boy.

Without thinking, he grabbed Opie, shoved his camera and bag into the kid's hands and literally threw them both into the passageway before the last beam cracked and fell. Slashing dirt slid over his forehead and caught in his nostrils, so he leaped back. There was a huge rush of earth in front of him. And then…only silence.

Luke could see nothing, only yawning, gaping darkness. His heart beat faster, and for the first time, panic and hot sweat slithered over him. He was trapped. *Trapped.* He had never felt so helpless in his life.

He reached out, pounding his fists against the solidly packed earth. Only moments before that had been a doorway into the light, into the world. Now it was a wall. And his blows made no impact whatsoever.

"Hello!" he cried, still pounding. "Anyone? Can you hear me?"

His own words echoed eerily. But there was no response.

He turned. Only darkness. Swallowing, he waited, expecting his eyes to adjust. But nothing happened. Nothing broke the blackness. All black. All silent. All still.

He called out again. "Hello? Anyone there?" No answer.

In a burst of anger, he spun around and ran his hands madly over the wall, looking for a crack. But it was solid. He slumped into a sitting position against the impenetrable fortress of dirt.

He had never felt such heavy silence pressing in around him. There were no voices from outside, no reassurance to let him know that rescuers were on their way. No taps, no chug of machinery. No glimmer of light. Nothing.

He didn't know how long he sat there. Time had lost its meaning. Finally, after what felt like hours, he knew he had to try to move. He remembered the main room, with its passageway now so solidly blocked. But there had been other, smaller passages out of the main room. Opie's voice echoed in his brain. *Wonder where all these little tunnels go?* They were narrow and undoubtedly unsafe, but they had to lead somewhere. Farther into the belly of the earth? Or out into the light of day?

There was only one way to find out.

Any kind of action was better than sitting here in the dark lamenting his fate. Concentrating as hard as he could, he peered into the darkness. Which way to start? Half crawling, with one hand against the wall as his only guide, he stumbled across the cavern toward the painting of the bull.

And then he reached it. He didn't know how he knew it was there, but he did. It was as if the wall was warmer there, as if he could feel the life force of the bull pulsing under his fingers.

"You're losing your mind," he told himself harshly. But he didn't care. As if compelled, he slid his hands to the deep red handprints—the artist's signature, he supposed. He couldn't see them, but he could feel them. And he fitted his hands into the prints, sure even in the dark that his fingers matched the thick red outlines.

Blood pumped through his veins, stronger, surer, and he felt more alive than he could ever remember. "Think," he commanded himself. "Listen."

And somehow it worked. What had just a moment ago seemed like endless darkness began to open up before him. Now he could see small gradations of shadow and hear minute, imprecise sounds. If he focused, he could differentiate the various smells—the dusty wall behind him, the damp earth at his feet and perhaps the faint scent of water somewhere, not near, but somewhere.

He didn't think about it, didn't worry about what had happened when he pressed his hands against the paintings. He knew instinctively that there was something mystical and mysterious about the whole place, repelling intruders, yet offering him a lifeline. Had the cave changed? Or had he?

Moving forward, Lucas set out. There was no longer any question. If they weren't coming to rescue him, then he would have to rescue himself. Using the tools he had available—his mind, his eyes, his fingers, his ears, his nose—he would find a way out of this place.

He would find a way.

Chapter One

When she saw the morning paper, Gillian Quinn almost choked on her coffee. Lucas was back, damn his hide. And no one had bothered to tell her!

"Always the last to know," she muttered, then stood up so abruptly she knocked over her mug, spilling a wide pool of creamy brown coffee right over Luke's scowling face.

That scowl was so typical it made her smile. "He comes home a hero and he still looks like he has a chip on his shoulder," she noted dryly. But her mood quickly changed to indignation. "And then he goes and shuts himself away at Blackthorn Manor without so much as a word. The nerve!"

She sat back down and stewed some more, tapping a finger against the text. "'Lucas Blackthorn, award-winning photographer,'" she read aloud, "'continues to elude reporters and well-wishers.' Well, knowing Luke, that's no surprise, is it?"

Resting her chin on one hand, she read on, "'Three weeks ago, Blackthorn ducked the spotlight yet again as he emerged from a hospital in Rome. Blackthorn had entered the hospital briefly so that doctors could check on his health after his two-week ordeal trapped in a labyrinth below the ruins of an ancient palace on the island of Crete…'''

Gilly shook her head. "As if anyone in the world doesn't know *that* by now," she said impatiently.

The man was a certified hero, what with saving the little boy *and* throwing his camera to safety, thereby preserving the only photographs of the cave painting of the Minotaur. At least that was what the newspapers were calling it. Gilly thought it looked like a rather badly shaped cow, but the Minotaur it had become. Magic and mythic and all that.

She shook her head. Half the students in her third-grade class could draw better cows than that. But at the moment their art prowess was not important. Right now all she cared about was Luke.

Thank God he was okay. She might be angry with him for not contacting her, but she was still mightily relieved by this bit of news. *Luke, fine. Luke, home.* "I knew it," she breathed. "I knew it."

First there was the devastating news that he'd been trapped in the cave and was presumed dead. She'd vacillated between being too upset to watch and staring at CNN for hours on end, hoping for a miracle.

She'd felt it was impossible that Lucas was dead. Anyone but Luke. He might be a bit of a challenge, with his prickly independence and his stubborn refusal to do things her way, but he was still the most vital and alive person she knew. No way Luke Blackthorn was going out that easily.

But he had no family, so there was no one to call and share her hopes with. Or even anyone to pump for the latest desperate bits of information. No one except Abigail and Harry Fitzhugh, who took care of Black-thorn Manor during Luke's frequent trips abroad. Aunt

Abby and Uncle Fitz. Not that they were *his* aunt and uncle. No, they were hers.

Unfortunately her aunt and uncle had always been very protective of Luke, even when it concerned Gilly. *Especially* when it concerned Gilly. "As if they'd need to protect him from me," she scoffed. The very idea was annoying beyond belief.

But every time she called, Aunt Abby stubbornly maintained that she knew nothing more than the papers did. Not that that kept Gilly from calling—she was not someone who took no for an answer, especially when it came to Luke. He'd been a project of hers for too many years to lay off now.

But her aunt wasn't saying anything. She'd been quiet as a church mouse ever since Luke disappeared into that murky labyrinth. She'd kept her silence even after the wonderful reports that Lucas had miraculously survived—charting a twisted and heroic path through ancient caverns in complete darkness, with no sustenance other than a package of throat lozenges and a few sticks of Juicy Fruit gum, and staggering into the sunlight after everyone but Gilly had given up hope.

"I don't know any more than you do, dear," Aunt Abby had said just yesterday in a strained and wispy tone. Stern precise Abigail Fitzhugh, whispering. Gilly had thought that was odd at the time. "He's probably off on his next adventure," her aunt had continued. "But if we hear from him, you'll be the first to know."

Yeah, right! Meanwhile the paper was reporting that Luke had been home for two weeks, with Aunt Abby no doubt cooking up pots of chicken soup for him while she was lying to her very own niece!

Frowning, Gilly returned to the article, just to make sure she hadn't missed anything. "Blackthorn is reported to be in good condition…" it continued. She judged for herself, peering at the picture. A little thinner, a shade more disreputable-looking, but otherwise okay. That was a relief.

She traced her finger past the coffee stain and into the body of the story. "'He appeared to be in some discomfort,' his doctor stated guardedly. 'We have, however, found no physical cause…'"

She wasn't exactly sure what that meant. She did know Luke well enough to remember that he was never sick, hated doctors and had probably clammed up at the first sight of a stethoscope. That might well account for his "discomfort." She read on.

Blackthorn was spotted reentering the United States through La Guardia Airport more than two weeks ago. Although he was rumored to be somewhere in Manhattan, reports have now surfaced that he immediately boarded a flight out of town and has been secluded in a family home ever since. Reports of the location of that home have ranged from an island in the South Pacific to the Rocky Mountains.

"The reports can range all they want," Gilly said tartly. "He only has one family home, and I know good and well where it is."

Blackthorn has issued no statements to confirm his whereabouts or his future plans, other than a brief press release through his editor at IPB maintaining that he wishes to be left alone. Experts continue to speculate on how he managed to find a passage through the mysterious labyrinth, but Blackthorn has not elaborated.

How had he managed to find a way out? Gilly didn't need to talk to him to know the answer to that one. He was Luke, wasn't he? Give him half a chance and he'd find a way.

But mingled with her pride, Gilly also felt more than a bit of exasperation. If the reports were correct, Luke had been holed up at Blackthorn Manor for more than two weeks. All alone except for two elderly servants, acting like a hermit, hiding from life outside the manor walls. It was typical but hardly healthy.

Without wasting another minute, Gilly decided what she was going to do. She would march right up to Blackthorn Manor and pound on the door until he let her in. And then she would pull him, kicking and screaming if need be, back into the world where he belonged.

Okay, so he was a teenager the last time, but still…

Gilly well remembered the effort it took to drag Luke to school dances he wanted no part of, to push him into taking photos for the student newspaper and painting scenery for the summer play, and in short, to force him to embrace life whether he wanted to or not. Hadn't she set up his first date, entered his photos in the first contest he'd won, even filled out his college applications?

"I did it before and I can do it again," she said with determination, rising from the table, grabbing her coat and heading for the door. "If Luke Blackthorn thinks he can hide from me, he's got another think coming."

WHAT WAS THAT god-awful noise?

Lucas swore under his breath. The pounding coming from downstairs was enough to wake the dead. And that dreadful music! Surely Abigail and Fitz knew better than to make that kind of racket when he needed complete...

He stopped, focusing. It wasn't coming from downstairs. It was outside. The front walk, all the way out beyond the gate. He stepped back, faltering. This was devastating news. He hadn't realized he could hear *that* well. Sure, noises had bothered him immensely ever since he got out of the cave, but nothing so faraway. Plus, he'd had the house soundproofed, and that had deadened the normal sounds of traffic and pedestrians coming from outside the walls of Blackthorn Manor. Till now.

Was it possible his hearing was getting more acute, more painfully sensitive? "God, no," he groaned.

But he had no time for speculation. The front gate creaked open ominously, announcing a visitor. Every clomping footfall imprinted itself on his brain. And the music— God, it was caterwauling! Someone was attempting to sing and not doing a very good job.

He clamped his hands over his ears, but it didn't help. The words "Jeremiah was a bullfrog" came careering up, and he groaned loudly.

There were supposed to be surveillance cameras and silent alarms mounted on the gate so that no one could venture inside without someone in the house knowing. He stalked over to the front window, edging the heavy curtain aside just enough to see who had penetrated his fortress, who was creating such a disturbance.

He should've known. He closed his eyes for a second, leaning his forehead against the icy glass. But it didn't help.

She was just making the first curve, still a good two hundred feet away, and she was muffled in a heavy coat and hat. But the wayward red curls escaping from around the hat, the determined set of her shoulders, the forceful crunch of each footstep against the crisp snow and that dreadful song—it added up to one person.

"Gilly Quinn, as I live and breathe," he said darkly.

He would've recognized her even without his amazingly sharp eyesight, yet another charming side effect of his time underground. His eyesight, his hearing, his fingers, his taste buds, even his nose were all fine-tuned and turned up to maximum volume. He had hoped it would all fade in time, representing no more than a faint memory of how he'd survived the cave-in. But now it seemed his powers were only getting stronger. He might as well be a circus freak.

Damn. He turned away from the window, still wincing with the impact of her song. "Think, think," he commanded himself. But how could he think with "Jeremiah was a bullfrog" reverberating in his head?

"Think," he said again. "What are you going to do about Gilly?"

Interfering, well-meaning, I-have-a-solution-for-everything Gilly Quinn. If he told her that he'd turned into a freak, she'd be signing him up for some twelve-step program in how to deal with freakdom. And if he didn't tell her, if he pretended nothing was wrong, she'd pester him to death to get him out of the house.

He never should have come back to Blackthorn Manor. Not when Gilly was within a hundred miles.

"HELLOOO," GILLY CALLED out, trying to get a good whack at the clacker on the front door. The doorbell seemed to have been disconnected completely, while the knocker had been modified somehow. For as long as she could remember, Blackthorn Manor's front door had displayed a big brass lion's head that made a good sharp crack when you banged on it. This one sounded as if it was wrapped in felt or something, making only a subdued thump. "Now why would Uncle Fitz muffle the door knocker?" she mused.

Finally Gilly abandoned it and just used her fist. "Aunt Abby! Uncle Fitz!" she called out, pounding as hard as she could. "I know you're in there. Open up! It's cold out here."

After what seemed like forever, the big old door swung open noiselessly.

"Fitz," she said with relief. Before her uncle even had a chance to say hello she squeezed through the doorway under his arm.

She shrugged out of her coat, planning to hang it on the antique coat tree that had stood in this hall since time immemorial. Except now there was no coat tree.

"Oh," she said, blinking. The vestibule had always been a classy black-and-white affair, with polished tiles that clicked nicely under your shoes and a huge crystal chandelier dripping with light. Now there was no overhead light at all, and the color scheme had become soft gray, with thick carpet underfoot. She turned back to her uncle, handing him the coat and hat she had no place to hang. "Redecorating? I kind of liked it the old way."

"Gillian," he said sternly, if rather softly. "Stop right there."

Shaking out her red curls, Gilly just grinned at him.

Harry Fitzhugh, her mother's older stepbrother, was a bona fide sweetheart and always had been. His gloomy expression and rather overwhelming size might scare off lesser souls, but Gilly knew him too well to be intimidated. How could she be cowed when she remembered taking piggyback rides on his broad shoulders or pulling the brass buttons off his chauffeur uniform to play checkers with? She'd called him Fizzy when she was very small, and he'd never once complained. How frightening could someone named Fizzy be?

"Hello, darling," she said breezily, rising to her tiptoes to give him a kiss on the cheek. "You still owe me ten dollars from backgammon."

"Gilly—"

She didn't believe in shilly-shallying, so she got right to the point. "I'm here to see Luke." He opened his mouth, but she went right on, moving toward the wide curving front stairs as she spoke. "There's no point pretending he's not here, because I know he is."

Uncle Fitz tried to block her path, but she only gave him a pitying look as she sidestepped him neatly, her hand already on the carved wood banister. *First line of defense breached.* "You can either tell me where he is or I can find him myself, Fizzy dear," she continued sweetly. "But I'm not leaving till I see Luke."

"Don't be absurd." From the shadows of the second-floor landing, Aunt Abby's words came hissing down at Gilly. Abigail Fitzhugh was a head shorter than her husband, but a lot scarier. Right now her glare could've frozen water into ice cubes at twenty paces. "Luke isn't here."

"Of course he is." Her aunt started to argue, but

Gilly held up a hand. "Aunt Abby, you're whispering. Now tell me, when have you ever done *that?*"

Aunt Abby's face flushed. "Well, I, uh—"

"Don't bother. I figure all this silence is for his benefit—you're trying to create a restful atmosphere or something." As usual they were being overprotective. *Nobody should live in this kind of a tomb,* she told herself. Especially not Luke.

Gilly marched up the stairs, her footfalls making soft thuds on the thick carpet. Glancing down at her shoes, she considered how curious it was that everything seemed different from the last time she was here. The door knocker, the front hall and now the ancient Persian rug on the stairs, the one she and Luke had slid down more times than she could remember, the one that had gotten more threadbare with each rough-and-tumble game, had disappeared. "What is going on around here?" she asked suddenly.

Aunt Abby stood her ground. "Whatever do you mean?"

"I mean Blackthorn Manor hasn't been redecorated since before Luke's grandfather died. His parents were never here long enough to change so much as a light-bulb, and Luke certainly never cared about the decor." Gilly chewed her lip. "And now all of a sudden you're redoing everything, and you're going for plush wall-to-wall carpets and hardly any lights? I feel like I'm in a funeral home. What gives?"

Her aunt flashed a confused look at her uncle, who could only manage to shrug his massive shoulders.

"Gillian, you should leave well enough alone," Aunt Abigail whispered, drawing herself up primly. "Luke's not well, and he doesn't need this kind of disturbance. If he wanted to speak with you, he would've contacted you, don't you think?''

"Not well?" Her heart plummeted. "Is something really wrong? The newspaper said he was fine…" Her first reaction was to fly up the stairs to his bedside and check on him herself. But what if he was really ill? She hesitated.

"He's fine," Aunt Abby hastened to assure her. "Just a little fragile. I'm sure when he feels stronger, he'll—"

"Fragile?" Gilly stopped short. "Luke?"

"Fragile" was the last word she ever would have associated with Lucas Blackthorn. It was, in fact, entirely unbelievable. She narrowed her eyes.

"I need to see him," she decided quickly, and she raced past her aunt, tired of all the objections and speculation and verbal volleyball. *Second line of defense breached.* Whatever was going on with Luke she would judge for herself, and that would be that. "Luke? Where are you?" she called out. As she opened doors on the second floor, her aunt and uncle chorused, "Ssshhhh!" from behind her on the stairs.

"Luke, I need to see you," she announced loudly, poking her head into an empty bedroom. "It's me, Gilly."

"Like I might think it was someone else?" asked a dark, silky, dangerous voice.

She spun around. Her breath caught in her throat. Luke.

He was half a hall away, leaning in a darkened doorway, wearing a white dress shirt half-unbuttoned over black jeans, with his black canvas high-tops unlaced and his hands in his pockets. His dark soft hair was as rumpled as his clothes, and he was thin enough that she could see the hard angles of his cheekbones and his jaw. He was a little pale, but it only made his eyelashes seem blacker and thicker, his beautiful eyes even bluer.

God, he looked great. But then, he always had.

"We tried to stop her," Aunt Abby said. "But she refused to—"

No one was going to stop her now. "Luke!" she cried, racing down the hallway. Without thinking, she threw herself into his arms. "You don't know what a scare you gave us, Mr. Rushing-Headlong-into-Danger." She knew she was beaming, and he looked very startled. But she couldn't help it. Overflowing with affection, she gave him a healthy welcome-home hug. "It is *so* great to see you!"

Obviously the feeling wasn't mutual. He couldn't scramble backward fast enough. And he seemed shaken, strained, as every last bit of color drained from his face.

"Luke," she cried, reaching out for him.

But he retreated quickly. "No, please," he said, wincing, holding up a hand to fend her off.

"Are you...?" Gilly didn't know what to think. How could one little hug have rocked him down to his toes?

Touching him had affected her, too, the way it always did, making her feel a little light-headed, giving her a tingle. She'd gotten very good over the years at covering up just how Luke's physical presence tended to knock her socks off. But this reaction from him...well, this was a different kettle of fish.

"Are you okay?" she asked finally, dying to touch him again but afraid to.

"I told you he was fragile," Aunt Abby interrupted, wringing her hands. "*Now* will you believe me?"

He waved the housekeeper away. "I'm fine," he said carefully. He sounded a bit breathless and unsteady, but otherwise very sure of himself. To Gilly he muttered, "I have...I have something like a bruised rib. Nothing serious, but painful enough. So please don't touch me...like that again."

A bruised rib. It sounded so ordinary and reasonable. She tried to relax her jangled nerves. "Why didn't you say so? Of course I won't hug you."

"Mrs. Fitzhugh, I want to talk to Gilly." He motioned again for the housekeeper to leave, and Abigail finally departed, firing a last angry glance at her niece.

"Well, Gilly," he said softly once they were alone. He took a few steps back into the room behind him, still holding his arms tight to his body. "You were so all-fired determined to see me. You're seeing me. Happy?"

"No, of course not. That is, I didn't mean to hurt you or anything." She followed, peering at him. The big high-ceilinged room was shadowy and dark, difficult to maneuver in. As her eyes adjusted, she took a closer look at her surroundings. How very odd. "This used to be the ballroom, didn't it?"

"Used to."

Gilly sent him a mystified glance. "What are you doing living in the ballroom? And what is all this stuff for?" She motioned toward a series of tables cluttered with all manner of plants and leaves and small trees. "And why is it so dark in here?"

"As always, you're full of questions." Luke switched on an overhead light, but it glowed soft purple in the cavernous room. "Ultraviolet," he explained. "And I don't live here. It's just...a garden. A nocturnal garden. A new hobby."

"A nocturnal garden?" Was Luke playing with Venus's-flytraps or something? And was this supposed to reassure her? She shook her head stubbornly. "You were never interested in plants. I can't remember you ever even having a hobby."

He shrugged. "So I have a hobby now. Things change."

"Not that much, they don't. Come on, Luke, spill it," she demanded. "What's really going on with you?"

"Could you please keep your voice down?" Edgy, he backed away, around the other side of an exotic-looking potted palm. "There's nothing wrong with me, nothing to figure out. But I don't suppose you'll take my word for it, will you?"

She was still mulling over that "keep your voice down" crack. Her voice was raised a little, but not that much. Not enough for him to act as if she was shouting at him. "This is getting weird. I can't hug you, I can't talk to you...and you wonder why I want to make sure you're okay."

"Don't I look okay?"

She lifted her gaze. "You look...*fine*." She couldn't help it; the word just came out that way, almost on a sigh. At least it seemed to have amused Luke. There was a new spark of humor in his sizzling blue eyes.

He raised an eyebrow. "That good, huh?"

"Oh, stop being so egotistical." She couldn't hold back a small smile. "It's a no-brainer, Luke. I mean, you know what you look like."

"Gill, I just got out of a cave. I do know what I

look like and it isn't pretty." He looked at her speculatively. "I'll say one thing for you. You may be a royal pain in the butt, but you're loyal."

Her smile widened and she said lightly, "Loyalty, equality, fraternity—that's my motto. When you're on my list of pals, you're on forever. Which is why I'm here."

He swept her with a jaded glance. "And why exactly are you here?"

"To get you out of exile, of course."

"Gilly," he said in a quiet but extremely firm tone, "it isn't exile. It's a vacation. I needed to take some time off to rest and recuperate. My life hasn't exactly been a picnic lately."

"Oh, come on." She ran a hasty hand through her curls, sending them into even more disarray. "I know you, and your idea of rest and recuperation is to find the nearest war zone and start snapping pictures. Not hiding, not...suffocating. You should be out in the world, taking pictures. This isn't like you!"

Turning abruptly, Luke stalked to the other side of the ballroom. She followed, determined to keep up with his long loose strides. The first thing she'd noticed about him, at the grand old age of nine, was how smoothly he moved, how those skinny, banged-up legs of his could eat up turf like nobody's business. It had fascinated her then and it still did. Luke even breathed gracefully.

"See?" He held up a battered camera, pretending to aim it at a small pot of ghostly white blooms. "I haven't abandoned my camera. I'm just taking different shots."

"Of these weird plants? Why?"

"Listen, Gilly, I spent two weeks in a cave in the

dark," he said with obvious exasperation. "I got interested in what happens when living things are deprived of light, okay? Sort of a scientific exploration."

The cave. Nocturnal. *Ahhh...* "Aside from the fact that you're not a plant, that actually does make a warped kind of sense."

"I'm glad something finally does," he muttered. "Look, I'm really tired. You've seen me, right? You see I'm fine. So no more Gilly-on-a-mission, please?"

"I can see you're pale and cranky and you definitely need to get outside into the fresh air." But the light in his blue eyes remained stubborn and unconvinced. "Even your plants need *some* light, whether they're nocturnal or not. And so do you. Being cooped up like this can't possibly be good for you," she maintained. "It's like a mausoleum in here!"

Luke lifted a dark eyebrow.

"Okay, okay." She couldn't believe she was giving in this easily. "I'll leave for now, but we'll meet for dinner next week, all right? We can talk about old times, about St. Benny's—did you know it isn't St. Benny's anymore, only Benny's? Just up and lost its sainthood."

"I know, Gilly," he said dryly. "That happened five years ago. The archdiocese sold it to a group of lay investors just before you started teaching there, right? I was only out of the country for six months this last time."

"Ten months," she corrected absently, gingerly reaching out a finger to test the prickliness of a very ugly cactus with long skinny stalks. "What *is* that?"

"Night-blooming cactus," he told her. "It has a very nice fragrance. You want to hang around till midnight and see it bloom?"

"No, I don't think so." It really was ugly, if no pricklier than Luke in his current mood. Quickly she abandoned the awful thing and returned to her favorite subject. "Benny's is a great school, Luke, and we're doing some wonderful things there. You'd be so proud of your alma mater," she enthused, taking his free hand and giving it a squeeze.

Suddenly he looked pale and strained again. She knew she had a tendency to ramble on when she got on the subject of her beloved Benedict Academy, and if Luke really was tired, she didn't want to overdo it.

"But listen," she announced abruptly, taking a few steps back and narrowly missing impaling her bottom on a cactus frond. "We don't need to go into that right now. Dinner next weekend, okay? It'll be great. We can even go to the Tackle Box, that nasty little diner by the river you always used to like."

"I don't think so," he murmured. "There are reporters everywhere—all looking for me."

"Reporters be damned!" she said with spirit. "Luke, you need to get out of this place. It's not good for you to—"

"No," he returned flatly.

"The snow is beautiful," she tried. "The river is frozen and people are skating—"

"No, Gilly. No."

With a sigh she realized there was no way to convince him. "Okay. For now." She leaned up to give him a quick kiss, noting his wince in response. Could a kiss on the cheek affect a bruised rib? She frowned, suspicious all over again.

"Close the door behind you, all right?"

She left him to his Venus's-flytraps. Chewing the inside of her cheek all the way down the stairs, she gathered her coat from the banister before she stepped resolutely out through the front door.

Halfway down the walk, she spun around and gazed back up at the tall shuttered windows of Blackthorn Manor. "You may have gotten rid of me this time, Luke, but I'll be back," she said softly. "You need to get out of all that gloom and face the world."

She turned into the wind and began the long trek back across the river. "It's for your own good, Luke," she said stubbornly. "And we both know it."

Chapter Two

Gilly propped her feet on her desk, tapping a pencil on the armrest of her chair and gazing in the general area of the Friends of the Zoo calendar tacked to her cubicle wall. But she didn't really see January's polar-bear poster boy.

No, her mind was otherwise occupied.

With Luke. Whose scowling face adorned the wall right next to the polar bear, where Gilly had taped up the newspaper article about his return.

For the past hour of her free period, when she should have been grading papers and going over the lesson for her two-o'clock French class, she'd been staring into space, thinking about Luke.

She frowned at his handsome face. "Talk to me, will you?" No response from the tattered clipping. Typical.

But even if she didn't get an answer until her dying day, she'd still be convinced that something was very wrong at Blackthorn Manor. It wasn't the way Luke looked or talked, not even his weird plants or the darkened ballroom. No, it was more the hushed tones and chilly feeling, as if the whole house were sending out touch-me-not vibes.

Luke had always been independent, but not like this.

"Ms. Quinn?" someone asked from just outside the wall of her cubicle, breaking her concentration. "You in?"

"I'm in." Quickly Gilly pulled her legs off the desk and adopted a more respectable pose, one befitting her status as the school's sixth- and seventh-grade English teacher. Actually English was only the tip of the iceberg, since she also taught art to kindergartners through to sixth graders, and French, speech and drama to seventh and eighth graders. She had a very full schedule. "Enter."

"Just me, Ms. Q," offered Tony Fielder, one of her favorite students, as he poked his head and one scuffed-up sneaker around the edge of the doorway. "Sorry to bother you. But I need your keys."

"My keys? Aren't you a little young to take my car out for a test drive?" she teased.

Tony rolled his eyes, giving her an exasperated expression only another seventh grader would appreciate. "How am I supposed to know you even got a car, Ms. Q?" he asked in an aggrieved tone. "I never seen you drive. I just wanted the key to your apartment. I wanna, you know, finish the mural today. Like *now*."

Gilly raised an eyebrow, but she didn't really mind the attitude. For one thing, she was used to it. And for another, she liked slender, dark-eyed Tony. He wasn't one of her best students, but he had potential.

Although he was fairly small and showed no signs of sprouting, he was already a standout basketball player. At any other school he'd be getting recruited to play at one of the city's powerhouse high schools, with promises of spiffy gym shoes and warm-ups and whatever else they could throw at him. At the Benedict Academy, he got none of those things.

Instead, he got pushed to concentrate on book-learning, which he dearly needed, as well as a chance to pursue his real love—art. Gilly had spotted him in her third-grade class back when they were doing collages with yarn and old newspapers. Even in that environment she'd recognized his talent. And she'd been doing her best ever since to keep him motivated. At the moment that included commissioning him to smear paint all over her living-room walls in whatever way he saw fit.

"You want to paint now? Don't you have class?" she asked in a no-nonsense tone. She might like Tony, but she had no illusions about his willingness to skip class if he could get away with it.

"Nah, I don't got class. Mrs. Benadetti is taking my last-period science class to the planet...planetarium," he said slowly, picking his way through the long word. "And I ain't goin'."

"You ain't, huh?" she asked dryly. "Why not?"

"My ma don't want me to go," he explained casually, "'cause that planet place is right by where my dad works, and my ma, she don't want me seein' my dad because he got busted again. She got, like a restraining order and he ain't supposed to be within a hundred feet, and I guess maybe he would be if I went to the, you know, planet place. So I thought, as long as I don't gotta go there, I could go over to your place and finish the mural. I could maybe finish it today with a coupla good hours."

Whew. What a story, restraining order and all. Benedict Academy was full of them. If it wasn't Tony and his deadbeat dad, it was somebody else getting their windows shot out or switching foster families for the third time. Life wasn't pretty in the neighborhood of West Riverside, and try as Gilly might, there wasn't a whole lot she could do about it.

"Let me think about it," she said, making a mental note to call his mother and make sure everything was okay. The old Gilly would've gone running off to talk some sense into his rotten father, but she knew better now. Every kid at the school had a story like Tony's, if not worse, and there was nothing she could do but pull them through Benny's by hook or by crook and do her darnedest to send them off to college and a better life.

"I've always been there when you worked on the mural," she told him evenly. "I don't know about this, Tony. All by yourself? Is that really a good idea?"

"Aw, come on," he pleaded. "I ain't gonna do nothin'. You know me!"

Actually she did know him. He was a good kid, with a mom who did her best to instill solid values in her son. Gilly made up her mind quickly—she was going to trust Tony.

"I wanna finish the mural so's I can get paid," he argued. "I need the cash, man."

"All right, but only if you ask nicely, with no 'ain'ts' and no double negatives, and don't call me 'man.' What did you say? 'I ain't gonna do nothin'? Jeez Louise, Tony." She dug into her purse and pulled out her key ring, twisting off the right key and then dangling it in the air. "Come on, you can do it. You're in my English class, kiddo. I can't let you get by with that kind of talk."

"Okay, okay. I promise that I will behave myself

and not do anything that you would not want me to do," he said precisely.

With a grin Gilly tossed him the key. As he caught it neatly, she warned, "You by yourself, understood? No friends. Anything you mess up, you clean up, and if you leave before I get back, lock the door and drop the key off with my neighbor, Mrs. Mooshman. Got it?"

He nodded and started to go, but Gilly stopped him.

"I'll call Mrs. Mooshman and tell her you're going to be there this afternoon so she can look in on you. So don't think this is a party or anything."

"Uh-huh, I got it." But Tony swaggered a little as he left. Gilly shook her head. She hadn't seen an attitude like that since the days another seventh grader, one Lucas Blackthorn, had strolled his way through these hallowed halls.

"Jeez, will you look at the clock?" She grabbed the lesson book for her French class, but she hadn't even had a chance to get the book open before Suzette Dayton, the social-studies teacher who had just been appointed assistant principal, came running in, waving a sheaf of papers.

"I'm late to judge the sixth graders' dioramas of ancient Rome," she said hurriedly. "But I wanted to give you those articles I promised you about the casino project. Do you have your speech ready? Because you might want to work in a few of these numbers from Gamblers Anonymous. They're pretty impressive."

"Speech?" Gilly sat up, aghast. "Is that tonight?"

"Of course it's tonight," Suzette returned sharply. "The city council meets every other Wednesday at seven o'clock. I'll be there, and Principal Sheffield will, too. A whole bunch of the teachers and parents are coming for moral support. Don't tell me you haven't written your speech yet?''

"No, of course I haven't. But don't worry." Gilly stiffened her spine. "I could do this one in my sleep. I mean, this is beyond nuts. We've been begging for urban renewal for years. And finally they promise they're putting big bucks into the neighborhood, but for what?'' She was getting up a good head of steam now, and she rose from her desk, waving a fist in the air. "So they can knock down St. Benny's and half of West Riverside to put up a stinking casino and some sleazy bars? Well, if the mayor and his cronies think we're going to take that one sitting down, they've got another think coming!''

"You tell 'em!" Suzette said with a smile.

"I plan to." Gilly pulled her datebook closer and flipped it open. "Tonight at eight. Got it. Right now I have a French class, and then I'm heading home to make sure the place is still in one piece after Tony gets through with it. After that I'll go through your articles and make sure all my ducks are lined up. Don't worry, Suzette. By tonight I'll have enough ammo to flatten the bunch of them.''

"I hope so." Suzette sighed. "Otherwise I'm afraid the Benedict Academy is history."

Gilly sat back down. "I still can't believe they would let it go that far. I mean, this place is an institution. Plus, we're getting such good results. Finally. Last year, eighty-five percent of our seniors went on to college. Eighty-five percent—it's phenomenal! They can't bring in the wrecking ball now."

"Sure they can," her colleague said gloomily, "if it means a floating casino with hot and cold running cash. They'd sell every school in the city down the river for that.''

"Not this one," Gilly vowed. "Not this one."

With one last "Go get 'em!" Suzette dashed out as quickly as she'd arrived, beating the bell by about three seconds.

Gilly grabbed her French book and ran for the hall. She spared one last glance at Luke's picture. "Wish me luck tonight, Lucas," she called back to the photo. "It's your alma mater, too, you know."

GILLY STIFLED a yawn.

"Order. Order, please." A rather stern-faced man with slicked-down hair and an ugly brown suit pounded his gavel for the umpteenth time that night. "We're moving on, people. Please stay with us."

Oh, well. At least the noise from the gavel was keeping her awake in the stuffy close quarters of the council room. It was a dark masculine room, all heavy wood and massive brass fixtures. She hadn't seen this much paneling since before Aunt Gert's knotty pine rec room went up in a fire.

The council members, all male, sat behind a long, highly polished U-shaped desk, each with a little brass nameplate affixed to his place. No such grandeur had been wasted on the spectators' area—they were stuck in rows of uncomfortable folding chairs that had seen better days. Gilly was close to the front, in the designated speakers' section, while the rest of the detachment from Benny's had been squashed into the back.

Reporters and cameramen, who looked as bored and restless as anyone else in the crowd, pushed in from the sides. But so far they hadn't even turned on the cameras.

Gilly shifted in her chair and smoothed the skirt of her suit, careful not to snag her nylons on the battered chair. She'd barely had time to rush home and change clothes—into the most conservative outfit she owned—before racing back to face the city council. Tony was gone by the time she got home, leaving his bright pop-art mural unfinished, but looking very spiffy. Gilly smiled at the memory. She was going to enjoy having bright blue blobby people and big yellow stars all over her living-room wall.

The city council, she thought, could've used a little of Tony's magic to spruce up *this* place.

They were working through the agenda, one interminable item at a time, as evening wore on into night. The guy with the gavel announced item number fourteen—proposed airport noise restrictions—and Gilly pinched herself to keep her fighting spirit in good order.

The casino project was item fifteen. Next on the agenda. It wouldn't do to lose her edge from sheer boredom.

An old man with a wheezy voice had made his way up to the microphone and was now voicing his objections to the airport ordinance, going into copious detail about why the city councilmen were no-good crooks. The crowd tittered, while one rather large oily-looking man sitting in a comfy armchair next to the council table broke out in hearty guffaws. Gilly had no idea who he was, but she reasoned he must be someone important to rate a special chair. That and the thick gold jewelry were dead giveaways.

As Mr. Oily's jowls jiggled with mirth, Gilly began to feel very annoyed. If this was how they treated anyone who spoke out against the council, she figured she was in for a long night.

Nonsense, she told herself sternly. She sat up straighter. *They can make fun of me all night. Who cares? I have right on my side.*

Finally, after the mayor told the speaker his time was up, item fifteen was called. It was as if someone had suddenly switched on the juice in the room. TV cameras whirred on, their lights blazing bright and hot, and every reporter reached for her notebook at the same moment. Even the oily man leaned forward intently.

Gilly just waited. She knew the deputy mayor, the one who was in charge of the casino project, would speak first. Tonight the thin, nervous, bow-tied deputy would formally present his proposal, and they would all see just how far-reaching the implications were going to be. In other words, the Benedict Academy would read it and weep.

Only after the deputy had shown off his charts, graphs and beautifully rendered diagrams would those pro and con get a chance to speak. Two pro, two con. Gilly was the second con.

She concentrated on the big, splashy artist's rendering of the Lucky Lady riverboat casino, bobbing there next to sketched-in restaurants and nightclubs. They'd planned for a small amusement park, an arcade and a whole block of shiny new luxury condos.

All very pretty, until you realized there was a parking lot where the Benedict Academy now stood. And a garish shopping mall took up the block where Tony and his mom lived, where Suzette had her apartment.

Gilly felt her anger rise.

The deputy mayor went on in a pleasant, rather monotonous tone about the many benefits of the planned development, and Mr. Oily nodded smugly in agreement. But the deputy didn't mention where the people who lived and worked there now were supposed to go. All he said was that this "eyesore" would be removed. By eyesore, she supposed he was referring to the entire West Riverside neighborhood.

Gilly had expected this, but she hadn't been prepared to feel so attacked, so vulnerable. That yuppie dweeb had just called her home an eyesore. *If thine eyesore offend thee, demolish it,* she muttered.

Once the deputy was done, the mayor thanked him heartily. Then the mayor announced the first of the pro speakers. Although they should have been ordinary citizens, Gilly knew better when the jowly Mr. Oily rose from his seat, gave a cocky wave to the assembly and ambled over to the podium.

The mayor beamed. "It is my pleasure to present Ed Spivak, the developer and owner of Lucky Lady casinos. Ed, what is this? Your sixth or seventh boat?"

"Ninth," Ed said with fake humility.

"Ninth? You don't say." The mayor shook his head in amazement. "So you can see, ladies and gentlemen, Ed is abundantly qualified to tell us about the super impact this kind of deal can have on a city. Ed?"

It was all Gilly could do not to leap up and throttle the mayor *and* his pal Ed. Meanwhile Ed went on at length about the incredible amount of money a casino pumped into an area. He paid a bit of lip service to jobs and opportunity, told a few homey anecdotes about the towns his casinos had saved from poverty and despair, and then shook hands with each and every person at the council table.

He might as well have pressed bills into their hands as he went, Gilly thought indignantly.

The second pro spokesperson, a restaurateur who hoped to set up shop next to the river boat, offered more of the same, urging the council to adopt the proposal for the good of the city. By now Gilly's hands had curled into fists. One more self-serving piece of drivel and she'd be ready to scream!

Instead, the podium was turned over to a very sweet older woman in a flowered dress. She represented a church from the other side of town that believed gambling was a sin and anyone who voted in favor of a casino would burn in hell.

Spirited, but hardly convincing. Heck, if there was a casino in West Riverside, the stooges on the council would be first in line to "sin" there.

Finally Gilly got her chance. Taking a deep breath, she walked slowly to the microphone. "It strikes me," she began, trying to speak calmly and persuasively, "that I am the only one of the speakers tonight who actually lives in West Riverside."

She got nothing but a few frowns from the councillors. She persevered. "I seem to be the only one who realizes the devastating effect your proposal is going to have on the people who live and work in this neighborhood. And that's what it is—a neighborhood. Not an eyesore. Not something to be leveled so that you can build bright toys for tourists with cash in their pockets. A neighborhood. Of course, if you pass Mr. Spivak's proposal, there won't be a neighborhood there at all."

She was just getting started. With passion rising in her voice, she whipped out statistics about who exactly would be gambling there, about who exactly would profit. She glared at Mr. Spivak, who in her mind personified organized crime.

Saving the best for last, she closed with a reference to the Benedict Academy. "If you have your way, my student Tony Fielder will never be an artist. My former student Rosalie Gonzalez would never have made it to the Fashion Institute. Sam Amiro would never have gone to MIT. We owe it to the kids of West Riverside not to let that happen, not to tear down their school and their homes, but to build them up, instead."

The gallery burst into spontaneous applause, but the men of the city council looked bored and disinterested.

"Time's up," the man in the brown suit announced, his tone as flat and dull as every other time.

"Thank you, Miss—" the mayor peered at his list "—Haversham."

"That was the first woman to speak," Gilly said, steaming. "I'm Gillian Quinn."

"Yes, well, thank you, Miss Gwenn."

"Quinn."

"Uh-huh." Absently he turned away, already dismissing her. "Are we ready for a vote?"

There was an audible gasp from the opponents of the casino. "You can't vote yet," Gilly protested. "A few comments and no real discussion, and you're going to vote?"

"You're out of order, young lady," the mayor said peevishly. "You had your say. Now leave it be."

Gilly stood her ground as catcalls and boos directed at the mayor came from the back of the room. "I will not leave it be. You people already had your minds made up before I even opened my mouth. The least you can do is explain this bizarre rush to vote. What are you afraid of? That if you give people time to discuss this, they'll see through your sleazy deal?"

"If you can't sit down and be quiet while we vote, you can be forcibly removed, you know."

"We're on TV," Gilly reminded him with a certain grim satisfaction as the reporters all began to scribble frantically. "Do you really want to forcibly remove me in front of the cameras? Do you really want to show the world what a bunch of bullies you are?"

"No vote! No vote!" her supporters began shouting in unison.

Their faces looking rather ashen, the mayor and his deputy put their heads together, joined after a moment by a sweaty Ed Spivak. Finally, as the noise level reached new heights, the mayor reluctantly announced, "It might be possible to table the proposal until our next meeting. I don't want to do that, because I really feel we've had plenty of discussion on this and the sooner we get going the better. But since you're so fired up about this, well, we want you to know we appreciate your concerns."

Gilly refrained from comment. *Appreciate our concerns, my eye. More like appreciate your own public image.*

"That'll give you time to get some community support," the mayor continued. "Because frankly, and I think I speak for the entire council when I say this, we haven't heard from one community leader who's against this, just a few individual malcontents."

Community leader? Doublespeak for people with clout. Teachers and parents—all the real people in the world—didn't count, just "community leaders." If Gilly hadn't already been furious, that would have put her over the top.

"Meeting is adjourned," the mayor declared.

Reporters began to converge on Gilly. She answered their questions as well as she could, trying to think "telegenic." Lord knew, they could use all the TV publicity they could get.

Finally the reporters had enough sound bites for the late news and they let Gilly go. She moved off to commiserate in a corner with Suzette and a small group from the Academy.

"Way to go, Gilly," the kindergarten teacher offered. "You didn't let them bully you."

"Yeah, well, that's all fine and dandy, but what do we do now?" Gilly frowned. "They're just delaying us, hoping we'll go away. And then they'll vote next time and this whole sleazy thing will slide right in. We need a few big-bucks types like that Spivak guy on our side."

"Don't count on it." Suzette sighed heavily. "Who do we know like that?"

"Someone with clout," Gilly said, thinking aloud. "Someone with a high public profile, money, influence... Someone who could take on the mayor and that creepy casino man." Her gaze narrowed. "I know someone who fits that bill."

"Who?" Suzette demanded.

"A bona fide hero who just happens to be a Benny's alum." She allowed herself a small smile. "Luke Blackthorn, that's who."

The home-ec teacher, a cute young thing, squealed, "You know Lucas Blackthorn? That gorgeous guy from the cave, right?"

"St. Benny's, class of '84." Gilly's smile grew wider. "Listen, everyone, I'll see you later. There's somewhere I have to go."

"Wait! Where does he live? Can I come along?" demanded the home-ec teacher, but Gilly just waved as she struggled into her coat and hit the road.

Time to beard the lion in his den. Again.

Chapter Three

This time the door opened before her hand even hit the knocker. And this time Luke himself answered.

Surprised, Gilly just stood there and stared at him for a minute. How did he manage to look so delicious, so tempting, so darn cool and collected, just by standing in a dark doorway?

"Unusually quiet for you," he said sardonically. "Isn't this a little late for a visit?" But he stood back and let her enter. In fact, he gave her a wide berth.

She figured the distance was because he was afraid she'd hug him again. Not likely after his reaction the last time. "Maybe I came to see your cactus bloom. Midnight, right?"

"Then I guess you're early."

"Okay, you got me," she admitted, stuffing her gloves into her pockets, pulling off her hat and stamping snow off her boots all in one flurry of activity. "I didn't come to see the cactus. I came because I need a favor."

"Is it the kind of favor where I come out to dinner with you for my own good?" he asked warily.

"No," she retorted. "I don't always sing the same tune, you know."

"Could've fooled me."

She gave him a stinging glare, the kind she gave her sixth graders when they misbehaved. "Can we talk somewhere besides the front hall? And not that black hole of a garden, either."

He seemed to consider a moment. "Is the kitchen suitable, Your Highness?"

"You really are in a mood, aren't you?" He didn't answer, so after a moment she said with exaggerated politeness, "The kitchen would be fine, thank you. Maybe Aunt Abby left us a cookie or two, hmm?"

"Sure, maybe." He led the way to the back of the house, his footfalls absolutely silent against the plush carpet.

How did he do that? The rest of the house was so quiet Gilly could hear her left heel squeaking slightly with every step. She could even hear her own breathing, coming a little unevenly after such a long walk in cold air. But Luke moved noiselessly.

The kitchen was warmer and cozier than the rest of the house, even though Luke left the lights off when they entered. But the big brick fireplace was lit, and its flames gave the room a lovely glow.

"This is nice," Gilly murmured, rubbing her hands near the fire. "She doesn't actually still cook in this thing, does she? Aunt Abby, pioneer spirit?"

"I don't know. I can't quite see her and Fitz hanging out popping popcorn over a roaring fire, can you?"

"Uh, no." She grinned, imagining her uptight aunt with a big hat and a black dress stirring some fearsome brew in a pot in the brick fireplace. "But you know, she'd look right at home tossing eye of newt into a big nasty cauldron."

"Abby? With a witches' brew?"

When Luke laughed, too, Gilly realized it had been a very long time since she'd heard his silky, slightly wicked laugh. She loved his laugh. She had forgotten how much. But here, in the hazy warm kitchen with Luke so close at hand, the sound of his laughter seemed to hit her in a different place. In the old days, she would've been delighted to hear him enjoying himself. Now the soft chuckle seemed to curl lazily inside her, sending sparks and tickles to all the wrong places.

Desire. For Luke. *Oh, dear.*

Gilly abruptly abandoned the fireplace and sat down at the kitchen table, folding her hands and staring at them, careful not to look at him while this...heat ran through her veins.

Lusting after Luke, even innocently, was a very bad idea. She knew that. Not only was he unattainable—and had always been unattainable—but he was her friend. Consciously bringing sex—even a little bit of sexual energy—into their relationship would send him running away faster than a jackrabbit. He'd spent most of his teen years eluding women on the make. Good heavens, she'd even helped him make his getaway on more than one occasion! But who would help him escape from *her?*

"Feeling guilty for calling Abigail a witch?" he joked, pulling out the chair across from her.

"Yeah, right." She gave him a guarded smile.

He folded his hands, too, mimicking her business-like pose. "And why exactly did you call this meeting, Ms. Quinn?"

"Funny you should ask." She took a deep breath, meeting his eyes with a great deal of hope. "I came here straight from a city-council meeting, Luke. I spoke out in opposition to the mayor's proposed plans to build a casino—''

''Whoa. Hold on a second.'' He pushed his chair back slightly, giving her an intent gaze. ''The mayor wants a casino in West Riverside? Last time I looked, gambling was illegal in this state.''

''Yeah, except for the racetracks, the lottery, off-track betting... Oh, and riverboat casinos.'' She couldn't keep the disdain from her voice. ''Don't ask me why it doesn't count if the thing is a foot offshore, but there you have it. And our fair city got one of the state's coveted permits, so they're bound and determined to bring in this cash cow.''

''Not exactly good news, but hardly a disaster.'' Luke stood and put his hands in his pockets. With the fire behind him, his hair had a soft bronze glow. Gilly found herself staring, until she had to tear her eyes away. She swore at herself under her breath. This was too important to screw up because she couldn't keep her eyes off Luke and his hair!

''Gilly, I didn't know you had that kind of vocabulary,'' he said with a touch of mischief. ''And why exactly are you having trouble keeping your, ahem, blasted mind on blasted business?''

She flushed. How had he heard that? Avoiding his question, she changed the subject back to the casino. ''Maybe it wouldn't be a disaster if they weren't planning to knock down half of West Riverside—excuse me, *all* of West Riverside—to make room for it.''

''So?''

''So—that's my neighborhood! That's where St. Benny's is.''

''Gilly—'' Luke began to pace impatiently in front

of the fireplace "—West Riverside is a dump. If they can clean it up, so much the better."

"I—"

"Hear me out," he continued. "For one thing, I can't believe you still live down there. It's a zoo! Knifings, muggings, drug dealers... Are you nuts?"

"No, I'm not nuts. I also work there. I grew up there. I went to school there. And so did you!"

"It wasn't as bad then."

"Baloney." She stood, too, eager to defend her turf. She stabbed one finger into the scarred surface of the table for punctuation.

"Could you stop pounding the table, please?" He set his jaw. "I have a headache."

She curled her hand into a fist. Keeping her voice low and intense, she declared, "A lot of good people live down there, you know. And we are fighting to save our neighborhood. If you had one ounce of empathy or compassion in that stupid, gorgeous head of yours, you would help me."

"Stupid *and* gorgeous?" He cocked an eyebrow. "Interesting combination. You make me sound like a supermodel, which is something I've never been accused of before."

"Just stupid," she grumbled.

There was a long pause. "So what was it you wanted me to do?"

"Join me and my friends."

"I'm not joining any crusades." Luke ran a hand through his hair, looking very weary. "The people who build casinos don't fool around, you know. They are not nice people."

"You don't have to fight them," she promised. "We just need your name, to let people know that someone like you is on our side. It will help a lot. You could give us some money—for St. Benny's, for a scholarship in your name, maybe. And you could come for Career Day and the Snow Ball, the benefit dance."

"I can't—"

"You can think about it. Luke, you're a press agent's dream. We need you!" she pleaded, giving him her best sweet-and-sincere smile.

"You can use my name for a scholarship if you believe it'll help. And I'll think about the rest." He held up a finger. "Just think. Nothing else."

"Luke, that's great! I promise you won't be sorry!"

Thrilled, she danced around the table to show Luke how grateful she was. But he backed off immediately, scrambling to get out of her range. Confused, she went sideways, intending to reach up and give him a very small, very harmless peck on the cheek. Instead, he feinted left just as she went right, and then he turned his head just as she planted one on him.

Oops. Right on the lips. Right on the hotter-than-a-pistol, hard, sweet, luscious lips. And this was no peck. This was a searing, sizzling slice of pure bliss.

Gilly fell backward, dazzled. He looked like he'd been blindsided. She understood the feeling.

"Sorry," she mumbled. Gathering up her coat and hat, Gilly couldn't get out of there fast enough.

Cold air smacked her in the face, but it was almost a relief. Ever since she'd met Luke, she'd tried to act cool and unconcerned, determined not to make a fuss over him like all the other girls did.

Yet here she was at this late date playing the fool.

"Aw, jeez," she said miserably, heading for the bridge back to the other side of the river. "Why did I do that? And why did it have to feel so damned good?''

LUKE STAGGERED upstairs to his bedroom, his mind and body reeling.

Obviously he'd been kissed before, but never with this kind of mind-shattering intensity. Damn his stupid body for blowing a simple kiss all out of proportion, for making him feel like his brain was buzzing, his lips burning, his fingers tingling, his ears ringing...

He fell onto the bed, wanting to wrap himself in thick layers of wool and never come out. Too much information was racing through his nervous system, sending impulses every which way. And suddenly one leg began to twitch. It would've been funny if it wasn't so humiliating. He felt like some kind of robot with all the wires crossed.

Taking several deep breaths, he focused hard to calm the racing of his heart.

Slowly, carefully, he closed his eyes, breathed deep and reeled in all his powers, turning down the volume for a while. He could do it if he concentrated. He'd been practicing, and he was getting better at damping down his infuriating supersenses.

All this was still so new, still so untested. It took several long moments for him to hear himself think again. Much longer than it had ever taken before.

But then, he hadn't been coming off a kiss from Gilly any of the other times.

He swore so loud it echoed in his ears. How strange. He turned his head toward the window. With all the commotion going on in his brain, he hadn't heard Gilly leave. No roar of an engine starting. No slam of a car door.

Luke paused, sitting up. Come to think of it, he hadn't heard any of the telltale sounds of an automobile when she'd arrived, either. Just the crunch of her shoes in the ice-crusted snow, the creak of the gate, the puffs of her breath.

"She was walking," he muttered. "Damn it. She was walking."

Quickly he strode to the window, slamming open the French doors and stepping onto the balcony. He gripped the railing, breathing deep of the dry, frosty air, gazing out across the river to the mean streets of West Riverside. The cold air pricked at his nose and his skin, but he ignored it, intent on what he was trying to do.

His house was high on the bluff, with nothing between him and Gilly's neighborhood but the frozen river. So close, and yet a world away.

"Damn it," he said again, more fiercely this time. He knew he was just venting his frustration, but somehow it made him feel better. "First she mouths off at the mayor and some casino sleazebucket, and then she walks home, at night, in the dead of winter, back to that lousy neighborhood where she lives. She might as well paint a target on her back!"

His words ebbed away in the cold, still air, leaving him in silence. But as he purposely fine-tuned his ears, reaching, stretching, for some evidence of Gilly's presence, he began to pick up sounds. There was a kind of hush, for the snow muffled many of the normal night noises. But he could hear the whistle of the icy wind sailing past his face, hear it skate over the frozen river below, hear the horn of a taxi not too far away, even the tinny footsteps of someone marching across the high narrow bridge that spanned the river.

Gilly. He knew it was her. It wasn't something he could explain, but his senses seemed even sharper as he honed in on his target. His gaze caught her small figure tramping resolutely across the bridge, head down, hands in pockets. Not even a car broke her path or lit her way.

Luke concentrated harder, astonishing even himself when he caught the subtle scent of her perfume. He remembered the smell from earlier in the kitchen, when he'd noticed the aroma of lavender that seemed to cling to her hair. Surely she was too far away for him to smell that now. But he did, as if the light fragrance was wafting on the wind directly from Gilly to his nostrils.

"This is impossible," he murmured. But he could see her, couldn't he? And hear her, almost taste her? As powerfully as he sensed her, Gilly should've been within a few feet. Instead, she was more like a mile away.

His powers were much stronger than he'd had any reason to know. But this wasn't some general bionic-man stuff. No, this was specific to Gilly. If there were other people on the bridge, he couldn't see them. If there were other men or women on the street outside Blackthorn Manor, their secret scents were safe from him. But Gilly was coming through loud and clear.

Could this be because of the kiss? As if she'd left a mark on him that he could use to pinpoint her presence?

He shook his head. "It can't be. There has to be some other explanation."

But he couldn't think about that now. As he traced her path, blocking out any other sounds or smells that might've interfered with his surveillance, he realized he could stay with her. It was as if he'd put a homing device on her, for God's sake.

The shadows deepened on the bridge, but he could still make out her small form, still hear every step, still smell that damned perfume or shampoo or whatever it was. And then she left the bridge, and her footfalls changed from a sort of ringing metallic noise to a softer sound against snow-deadened concrete.

She turned down a street in West Riverside, and he lost visual contact. "At least I can't see through buildings," he said, almost glad to know his powers had a limit.

He narrowed his eyes. He might not be able to see her, but he could still hear the telltale rhythm of her footfalls. And they had stopped.

He flared his nostrils slightly, breathing deeper. His nose was picking up a new odor. Fear. His brain recorded the data quickly, with one piece of information tumbling after the other. Sweat. Unwashed bodies. *Fear.*

His heart pounding, his mouth dry, he could physically feel the tension radiating from wherever she was. But it wasn't her fear—it was *his.*

"I'm scared to death she might be in danger," he realized. And his own fear was coloring his perceptions. He swallowed against the panic, calming himself enough to reconnect with the faint ribbons of sound coming from below.

A clatter of voices, Gilly's among them. She sounded calm, soothing. Good for her.

But there were other sounds, too—a squeal of protest, heavy footsteps, the harsh clank of metal, angry threats—drowning her out.

He pushed his powers further, closing his eyes, concentrating on the pattern of noises. But it was too muddled, too confusing.

"Damn," he said, pounding his fist on the wrought-iron railing of his balcony. His muscles didn't respond well to quick violent movements like that, and they sent him a nasty throb of agony. Every interaction with the outside world seemed to bring only one thing—more pain.

But he knew what he had to do.

"There's only one way to make sure she's safe," he said grimly. "I'm going to have to go down there."

GILLY TRIED to stay calm. Defiantly wielding a garbage-can lid with one hand, she shoved Tony further behind her with the other.

"Stay back," she hissed over her shoulder.

"But you—"

"I'm covered," she argued, brandishing the big metal lid like a shield.

"We gonna get you, lady," one of the punks taunted, slashing out with his knife just for kicks. He was at the other end of the dark alley, nowhere near her, making ninja motions to act cool. "We gonna get you and your little girlie friend, too."

Tony made a growling sound deep in his throat, and Gilly sent him a scathing glance. Now was not the time for macho heroics. But trust a teenage boy to get all bent out of shape because some nutcase criminal threatened his manhood.

"You guys are pathetic," she shouted, kicking a trash can and making a nice loud bang that she hoped would wake up a few neighbors.

"You one weird broad," the other thug accused. "You crazy, lady, interfering like this. You coulda just walked on by, y'know?'' Although he displayed a somewhat rational streak not shared by his compatriot, he also seemed to be taking it personally that she wasn't cooperating and letting them slice and dice her student without complaint. ''You gonna be very sorry you screwed with us.''

''Yeah, well, next time maybe you should pick your target a little better,'' she retorted. ''No way I'm walking on by when lowlifes like you two start ganging up on friends of mine.'' To Tony she added darkly, ''Even friends who have no business being out this time of night.''

Punk number one, the mouthier and less grounded in reality of the two, let loose with a stream of invective that centered on bodily functions, waving his knife and lurching closer. Too close for comfort. Her heart beating a little faster, Gilly edged back a step, pushing Tony toward the end of the alley where he could maybe escape. To cover her egress, she clanged the garbage-can lid back and forth on the side of a building. ''Help!'' she cried loudly. ''Anyone! Help!''

''Hey, what's going on?'' A pretty blonde in a trench coat appeared in the alley. She looked nervous, but she held up a miniature canister on a key chain. ''I have mace!'' she announced. ''So you guys better back off.''

Without comment, Punk number one let out a fearsome yell and reached out as if to smack her. He didn't actually make contact, but the woman slipped on one of her smart little pumps and crumpled to the pavement, sending her tiny can of mace skittering into the shadows. And then she started to whimper. So much for the cavalry.

''I'm tired of this crap!'' Punk number one shouted,

glaring at Gilly. Punk number two pulled out his own blade and started advancing. Grimly Gilly judged her chances with each of them. Her trusty shield couldn't protect her on both sides at once. So who should she go for—Mr. Erratic-but-Scary or Mr. Controlled-but-Threatening?

Just as she gritted her teeth and made up her mind, yelling, "Run, Tony!" and giving him a shove backward, a bizarre figure loomed over the scene from the blackest corner of the alley.

He was tall and kind of spooky, swathed in a long black coat that made his shape hard to determine. Wide shoulders definitely, but the rest was impossible to tell. His collar was raised, and his features were concealed behind a dark scarf that wrapped around his face like a bandit's mask. A black fedora was pulled down low over his forehead. Very dashing. Very Humphrey Bogart.

Just under the brim of the hat, Gilly caught the reflection of sunglasses. He was wearing sunglasses? At night? In the deepest shadows of a dark alley?

"Where did you come from?" Gilly whispered as the man in black swept down on the two thugs.

It was too dark, and it all happened too quickly to be exactly sure what he did, but as Gilly stood there, her trash-can lid dangling from one hand, the tall man crashed Punk number one into a brick wall and then knocked the knife out of Punk number two's hand. The second one seemed to consider a moment, gazing back and forth between his injured hand and the moaning heap that used to be his partner.

After one last four-letter word, he took to his heels and ran.

Suddenly all hell broke loose. Tony scrambled back

into view, the blonde sat up and started to shriek, and the sharp piercing squeal of a whistle penetrated the alley.

It all sort of swirled around the edges of Gilly's consciousness as she stared at her rescuer. "Wh-who are you?" she asked, peering into the shadows for a better look.

In a soft, dangerous voice, he whispered, "You'd be advised to stay off the streets."

His words and the sheer power of his presence spun out and looped around her, lashing her, pulling her toward him. It was as if nothing else existed in the alley but her—and him.

Her mouth dropped open. She took a step back, coming flush up against a wall. She never would've believed it was possible to be burned by the heat of a gaze she couldn't see, or to get all tingly and turned on by someone who hadn't even touched her.

But he was so tall, so intense, so overwhelming, that all it took were a few whispered words, and she was positively adrift in desire. How did he do that?

Behind her Tony whispered, "That dude's awesome, man," just as another earsplitting whistle sounded, so close Gilly winced and spun around.

Blinding light hit her right in the eyes. Squinting and shading her gaze, Gilly took a gander at the cause of the commotion. "Mrs. Mooshman! And Mr. Zamechnik!" Two neighbors from her building? They were wearing bright green jogging suits and toting heavy-duty flashlights and whistles. "What are you doing here?"

"We're on NOD patrol tonight, darling," Mrs. Mooshman said happily, giving another good blast on the whistle.

"NOD patrol?" Gilly was afraid she was going deaf. Smiling sweetly, she reached over and put her finger over the hole in the whistle. That solved one problem.

"Neighborhood Observers and Defenders," Mrs. Mooshman supplied, tapping the letters embroidered on her ghastly green jacket. "The NOD Squad. There was a sign-up sheet in the laundry room last week, and I said to myself, Iris Mooshman, you need to do that, even though I didn't know I would get this imbecile—whose name shall remain nameless by me, if you get my drift—for my partner." She gave poor Mr. Zamechnik, who was eighty if he was a day, a jab with her elbow. "Because this imbecile takes much too long and he also cannot read a map. So it's a good thing he has me as his partner, because otherwise, I swear, Gilly darling, we would still be back in the lobby of 104 Beech Street, which is where we started of course, trying to figure out where to go—"

"Oh, dear," Gilly interjected helplessly. She knew Mrs. Mooshman would go on for hours if they let her.

But the punk on the ground began to stir, sitting up and groaning loudly, so Mrs. Mooshman toddled right over and bonked him on the head with her flashlight, and he went down like a sack of potatoes.

Mr. Zamechnik asked politely, "Should somebody maybe stop the blonde girl from screaming so loud? Would you like I should slap her or something?"

Gilly shook her head hastily and went to help the woman, who was still sitting where she'd landed, her hands over her mouth, yelping in sharp little bursts. "It's all right now," Gilly told her soothingly. "You're fine. I don't think you're hurt. Unless you twisted your ankle or something when you fell."

The blonde stopped in midwail, looked Gilly right in the eye and cried, "I ran my nylons. And I broke three nails!"

"Gee, that's awful." Probably in shock, Gilly decided charitably. She dusted off the blonde and helped her to her feet and then started back to check on Tony and the two senior-citizen avengers, but the woman grabbed her arm.

"Hey, who was that guy? You know, the one in black?"

Gilly whirled ground. She gazed into the shadows where he'd been. "I guess... I don't know."

Gone. He was gone. As swiftly as he'd appeared, he'd vanished. Too bad. She still had this funny twinge in her stomach just remembering the way he'd looked at her from behind those glasses. And she would've liked to get a better look, thanked him properly...maybe get his phone number.

Meanwhile quite a crowd had gathered.

"Gilly dear," Mrs. Mooshman called gaily, "the mayor's here! He wants to talk to you, and so do some of these nice reporters. They're going to put our names in the paper."

"Hey, wait just a second." The blonde pushed past her. "I'm a reporter, too, and this was *my* scoop!"

"Hey, Devon," one of the other guys called out, "what happened, anyway?"

And before Gilly knew what happened, Devon Drake, girl reporter whose mace had not saved the day, had become the heroine of the story. It seemed a whole gaggle of reporters had been accompanying the mayor on a trip through West Riverside, so His Honor could point out how dangerous the neighborhood was at the same time he showed them where the riverboat casino would go.

And now they'd all stumbled on the story of the year, wherein the plucky girl reporter was mugged in an alley and a tall, handsome good Samaritan came flying in to save her. Gilly noted that the part about Ms. Drake cowering in the corner nursing her broken nails got left out somehow.

Tony was commandeering a couple of reporters of his own. "It was just like Batman. I mean, the dude—he, like, dropped out of the sky. It was so cool. No, wait, more like that immortal guy on TV—what's his name? The one who wears a long black coat because he cuts people's heads off and hides his sword under his coat?"

The reporters all looked mystified, but they dutifully recorded every word.

Gilly gave one last glance around, but there was no sign of her mysterious rescuer. Batman? An immortal with a sword? Somehow she figured it was some regular Joe in his winter coat and scarf. It was bitterly cold, after all.

"Can you give us a description of this man, miss?" Somebody shoved a microphone in her face.

"I don't know. It was very dark." She threw up her hands. "Long black coat. He had a hat and a scarf. Oh, and sunglasses."

"Sunglasses? Are you kidding?"

"Nope." Gilly drew upon her mental picture. It was so vivid she shivered inside her coat. "He was definitely wearing sunglasses, the really dark kind." She shrugged. "That's all I know."

"Yeah, I forgot that," Tony chimed in. "Dude was wearing shades at night, man."

Gilly felt the weight of her day descend on her all at once, and she gathered up Mrs. Mooshman and Mr. Zamechnik and then strong-armed Tony into coming with them. "We're walking you home first, buddy boy," she told him with a rather severe look.

They left Devon Drake in the alley behind them hobnobbing with the mayor, as their little group marched homeward. Mrs. Mooshman was gabbing the whole way, but Gilly didn't hear much of it. All she could think about was the man in black.

This was the first time in her entire life she'd been a damsel in distress and someone strong and dishy had actually rescued her.

What a day.

Chapter Four

Luke fled back to his car, feeling pulverized by all the sounds and sights and smells he couldn't quite filter out. God! That woman with the whistle—and the other one who kept screeching! His head was pounding and buzzing at the same time.

Well, at least Gilly was safe. He smiled, even though it hurt his lips. But the mental picture of her and her garbage-can lid was one for the books. If only she hadn't been clanging it around quite so loudly.

Carefully he removed his protective earplugs, tossed off the cashmere scarf and the old hat of his dad's and then slumped behind the steering wheel, too fried to drive just yet. His big old Cadillac with its shaded windows was quiet as a tomb, and slowly his breathing returned to normal, and the freaky snapping and popping in his head subsided. But he couldn't quite lose the overwhelming sensations of Gilly.

With his adrenaline running on high, he'd zeroed in on her like nobody's business. His nostrils were filled with her, his eyes drank her in, his very blood pulsed with her essence, and every nerve ending in his body went on red alert. It was amazingly intimate. And amazingly painful.

Wearily he started the car with a shaky hand, aware he had to get back to the safety of the manor before he got caught. All he needed was more publicity. He could see the headlines—Freak Photog Turns Vigilante. Bionic Bully Busts up Muggers, Limps Home.

Yeah, it was great.

The Caddy glided back to Blackthorn Manor almost by itself, thank goodness. He'd always hated the family fleet of mammoth black sedans, preferring something racier and more fun. But now he was glad to bury himself in this one, with its thick windows and steady, noiseless ride.

He pulled it into the garage, surprised to find Fitz up and waiting for him.

"Sir," the chauffeur said disapprovingly, standing there in his pajamas and robe, "you'll forgive my saying so, sir, but you should not be out. Not in your condition, sir."

"I didn't have a choice."

Fitzhugh eyed his attire. "Something to do with Gillian, sir?"

"You might say that."

"How unfortunate, sir," the big man said mournfully, twitching his mustache. "Perhaps next time I should be the one to deal with Gilly, as she is my niece. Especially given your condition, sir."

"I can't hide inside this mausoleum forever," Luke returned. It would've sounded more convincing if he hadn't come out of the car staggering like a drunk.

Fitz made a tsking noise. "Where did you get these clothes, sir? Not your usual style."

"It's your coat, Fitz," he informed his chauffeur. "Sorry about that. At least it's an old one. I found it and the hat in the storage room. I think the hat was my father's.''

"The storage room? Been in the secret passage again, have we, sir?''

Luke attempted to maintain his balance as he peeled off the coat and handed over the other items. "If you would be so kind as to return these things to the storage room, Fitzhugh.''

"Of course, sir.'' He cleared his throat meaningfully. "And if you don't mind my saying so, sir, next time perhaps you should consider waking me so that I might drive you.''

"I've got to find a way to control this myself,'' Luke said harshly. "Being driven around like a society matron won't help. If I have a hope of going back into the world someday, I have to get stronger and regulate these damn powers better. I have to.''

"Yes, sir.'' Fitz offered a discreet arm to help him into the house, where Abigail was waiting.

"You look awful,'' she whispered. "You can see how much good it did you to get out into the fresh air. Maybe this will convince you to pay no attention to what Gilly says.''

"Maybe.'' He cracked a smile. "But probably not.''

And so the three of them, an odd little party, made their way upstairs to Luke's room. Although he felt as if he'd gone ten rounds with the world heavyweight champ, he knew this wasn't a case of physical aches and pains.

"I'm going to try the sensory-deprivation tank,'' he announced. "My senses could stand a little deprivation at the moment.''

Rigid with determination, he flipped open the lid

and lowered himself into the tepid gray tank. *Control. Relax. Turn down the volume. Mind over matter.*

It had to work. But if it didn't, what could he try next?

ALL ANYONE COULD talk about was the man in black.

As Gilly tried to gulp down a cup of coffee in the teachers' lounge, the room was abuzz.

"I heard he was, like, seven feet tall, so they think he must be a professional basketball player," one particularly gullible woman offered. "You know, the Chicago Bulls were in town last night. Do they have any seven footers?"

"Seven feet tall?" Gilly just laughed.

"They're calling him the Riverside Samaritan, have you heard?" The bubbly young home-ec teacher was practically beside herself with excitement. "I watched Devon Drake on the news this morning. She said she would've been dead for sure, because the six guys who attacked her all had knives and guns. The Westside Samaritan did karate or judo or something."

"Six attackers?" Gilly rolled her eyes.

"My morning paper called him the Alley Cat, not the Samaritan," a no-nonsense coach put in. "They're theorizing that he has a rare eye disease—hence the dark glasses."

"Well," Gilly interjected, picking up a different paper from the three or four that littered the table, "this one says Streetwise Knight. And this other one says Riverside Rescuer. They're all ridiculous, if you ask me."

"I heard he was blind, and the kung fu was all by smell!" the wide-eyed home-ec teacher added.

"You were there, right, Gillian?" the Bulls fan

asked. "Tony Fielder was telling a group of kids this morning that he was there first and you came later."

"Yeah, I was there." Gilly stood, gathering up all the papers so she could throw them away. "It was no big deal, okay? Or it wouldn't be if the papers weren't treating it like the nail in West Riverside's coffin. Did you see this?" She held up the most objectionable one. "'Mayor Malone calls West Riverside the most dangerous place in the city. "Something must be done!"'" It's enough to make you lose your lunch."

The others stared at her for a few seconds, and then went right back to gossiping about the seven-foot karate expert with cataracts.

Gilly listened ruefully. It all would've been incredibly silly if it wasn't for the fact that he *had* seemed like someone extraordinary. Not a giant, not a kung fu master, not someone with X-ray vision. Just a man. Albeit a very *potent* man.

She shook her head to clear the cobwebs. Funny how it all seemed like a dream now when at the time it had been the most vivid experience of her life. Maybe danger did that to you. Made time stand still, made people seem a lot sexier and stronger and—

"Hey, how did it go last night?" her friend Suzette asked, heading off Gilly's fantasies at the pass.

"Last night?"

Suzette gave her a funny look. "You know, with Lucas Blackthorn. You were going to go ask him to sign on to our campaign, right?"

"Oh, yeah, right." She had almost forgotten about Luke with all this brouhaha. "It went fine." And then she remembered. "Except for the fact that I sort of kissed him by mistake."

Suzette's eyes were round. "You *what?*"

Gilly waved it off. "It was no big deal. And besides, it happened after he agreed to let us use his name, so it doesn't matter. I also broached Career Day and the Snow Ball—oh, and a scholarship fund—so I guess I'd say it went very well."

"Okay, if you say so." But the assistant principal looked as if she was trying hard not to laugh. "Listen, I'm going to go run off the sign-up sheets for a rally against the casino. You want to draft a press release with Blackthorn's name in it to send out today? I mean, I wouldn't want all that lip action of yours to go to waste."

"Suzette!" Gilly protested, but her friend was already wending her way out of the lounge, looking very smug.

Lip action. *Really.* One stupid little smack that hadn't meant anything to either of them. Had it?

Gilly decided to get out of the lounge while she still had her sanity. All this West Riverside Samaritan talk was making her balmy. Too bad that as soon as she swung open the door into the hallway, she ran right into Devon Drake.

"Hi!" the blonde said brightly, clicking on a small tape recorder and pushing it at Gilly. "You're just the one I was looking for. Can I talk to you for a few minutes?"

"Did you get your fingernails fixed?" Gilly asked just as brightly.

"Oh, uh-huh. Thanks for asking."

Doesn't even get it. Gilly shook her head. "Listen, I would love to talk to you about how wonderful the Benedict Academy is, as I'm sure you can see if you look around you. Or about how devastating the mayor's proposed casino project will be to this neighborhood. There's a great story in that.''

Devon screwed up her pretty face. "I don't think so. But, hey, what can you tell me about Nightshade?''

"Nightshade?" Gilly kept walking toward her classroom. "You mean the guy in the alley?''

The reporter nodded eagerly. "Nightshade is the name that seems to have stuck. Good one, huh?''

"I hadn't heard it before. Who comes up with these things, anyway?''

Tony Fielder popped up at the right moment to answer that particular question. "Hey, Ms. Q!" he called out, getting into step on the way to her English class. "That was me! Good job, huh? Dude wore shades at night. Nightshade, get it?''

"Yeah, Tony, that's great.''

"So who is this Nightshade character?" Devon asked in a conspiratorial tone. "Do you have any clue about his real identity?''

"Not even a hint of a clue. Sorry.''

"Don't you think it's odd that this tall dark *fabulous* stranger…'' Devon liked her own words so much she shivered.

Gilly was rapidly getting the idea that Ms. Drake was not so much driven by her nose for news as by a certain fascination for a pair of broad shoulders and a serious case of animal magnetism. She wished she could put her hands over Tony's ears; he was a little too interested in all this. But she knew he'd seen far worse than one amorous reporter in his young life.

"But seriously, Gillian," Devon said, leaning in closer, "why would this fabulous hero just come out of nowhere to save two women and a child and then take no credit for it? That is beyond weird, don't you think?''

Gilly paused at the door to her first-period classroom. ''Maybe he values his privacy.''

''It seemed like he knew you,'' Devon said thoughtfully, chewing her glossy lower lip. ''I just sensed this…connection between the two of you.''

How did you have time to sense anything from where you were cowering in the corner? ''No, there was no connection between us, and I have no idea who he is,'' Gilly said politely. She switched gears, giving the home team one last try. ''But if you'd like to talk about the Benedict Academy, I can guarantee you a wonderful human-interest story. We're in the business of saving young lives here every day. Not in alleyways, but in the classroom.''

''Not interested,'' Devon snapped. ''But if you hear anything about Nightshade, you call me, you hear? Night or day, whenever. Because I'm going to break this story wide open. Can't you just see my byline on the story 'Who is Nightshade—secret identity revealed.''' She shivered again.

''Good luck.'' Okay, so maybe she was wrong about the nose for news. Gilly pushed open the door, ushering Tony in ahead of her and firmly turning her back on Devon Drake.

''Take your seats, people,'' Gilly said loudly, facing twenty-five young students. All in their places with bright shining faces. Or close enough, at any rate. She perched on the front of her desk, opened the play they were studying—*Twelfth Night*—and smiled with encouragement and enthusiasm. ''Good morning, class.''

''Good morning, Ms. Quinn,'' they echoed in singsong voices.

"Today we start with act 2, scene 3." She looked up expectantly. "Who wants to be Sir Toby Belch today? Volunteers?"

Another day, another class. Another chance for control and order to prevail against chaos. In other words, nothing like last night.

"GILLY, ARE YOU about done?" Suzette was already in her coat, clutching a bulging briefcase, clearly ready to leave for the day. "It's almost six. I can give you a ride if you want to go home now."

Gilly pushed her chair back and stretched. "Wish I could. Thanks for the offer, but I've got way too much to do. I haven't even gotten to the press release yet."

"It can wait until tomorrow."

"Yeah, but it shouldn't." Gilly fixed a smile on her lips. "Don't worry. I'll get out of here sooner or later."

"Probably later." Suzette shook her head. "Listen, some of the juniors are cleaning up the gym to earn extra money, there's a Brownie troop in the kindergarten room, and the latchkey program is in the cafeteria till seven. So you're not alone."

"Benny's is never empty," Gilly returned lightly. Too many kids with no place else to go. No place safe, at any rate.

"You know, Gilly, after last night, you probably shouldn't walk home alone. These streets seem to be getting worse. Maybe you should—"

"I'll catch a ride with one of the teachers from the cafeteria."

"Good." Suzette waved one finger. "See you tomorrow."

Gilly immersed herself in her study plan for second-semester art classes, arranging and rearranging old plans to suit new shortages of supplies, as the minutes sped by.

The next time she looked up, it was past nine o'clock. There went the escort from the latchkey program. Rubbing her eyes, Gilly stood and collected the rest of her papers. She still hadn't gotten to that pesky press release, but maybe she could do it at home in front of the TV.

Whistling a few bars of some old song about sunshine and blue skies, Gilly let herself out into the main hall of the Benedict Academy. It was unusually quiet even for nine-thirty, with no errant kids milling around. Maybe some of the parents had begun to believe the bad press and were bringing their children home earlier.

"Hello?" she called out, sticking her head into the kindergarten room. But if a Brownie troop had been there, they were long gone. The gym was just as empty, although it did look well scrubbed, which meant the juniors had done their job.

She even tried the cafeteria just to be sure, but it, too, was silent and shuttered. "So I guess I'm walking, after all," she said out loud, her words echoing in the deserted hallway. No big deal. After all, she walked to and from Benny's every day.

She shrugged into her coat, pulled her hat down over her ears and hoisted her backpack onto her shoulder, preparing to meet the onslaught of cold air as soon as she hit the pavement.

"Brrr." It felt colder than she remembered, probably because the school was stuffy, and she moved briskly to create some body heat. Then she paused.

Standing there in the middle of the sidewalk, Gilly

waited, listening. How very strange. There was nothing she could put her finger on, but she had the distinct impression she was being followed.

She whirled around. But there was no one behind her, at least no one she could see. Frowning, she peered into the shadowed, snow-covered shrubs near the entrance to the school. There were enough dark spaces and black holes back there for a whole fleet of muggers to hide if they'd wanted to. But nothing moved, no one stirred. She waited for several long moments, until her feet were too frozen to stand still any longer.

"Whoever you are, go away!" she shouted. But her words blew away in a blast of winter wind.

Giving herself a quick pep talk, she moved on. But she couldn't shake the feeling that there were eyes directed at her back. Friendly or unfriendly? She had no idea. Either way, it was a creepy feeling.

She lived about six blocks from the school, and she practically flew all the way, refusing to slow down for patches of ice or hard-packed snow. Every funny noise, every shadowy tree branch, made her heart beat a little faster. It was unlike her to be so paranoid, but maybe she'd been reading a few too many newspapers about the crime rates in West Riverside.

She had never been so happy to see the lighted entryway to 104 Beech Street. Home. With another quick glance around, she fitted her key into the front door and jumped inside. Safe behind the glass door, she scanned the street for the person she simply knew was out there.

No one. Whoever it was, he wasn't drawing any attention to himself.

But she couldn't stop the anxious feeling that kept

nagging at her. She sped up the stairs, more than ready to barricade herself in her apartment. As she reached the third floor, she frowned. How long had the overhead light in her end of the hallway been burned out? She could still see, however, and she wedged the door to the stairs open to light her way.

But when she edged down the hall, she stopped dead in her tracks.

Light spilled through the crack around her door. And the door stood open about half an inch.

Someone was in there.

With all of her alarms blaring in her brain, she about-faced and went to Mrs. Mooshman's door, instead. "It's Gilly," she whispered through the door, positioning herself right in front of the peephole to give Mrs. M a good look. "Mrs. Mooshman, I think there's someone in my apartment."

The chain detached and the door flew open. "I'm ready!" proclaimed her neighbor, brandishing her NOD Squad flashlight like a club. She was wearing a housecoat and rollers, instead of her official Neighborhood Observers and Defenders green jogging suit, but she was still pretty scary.

"Maybe we should call the police," Gilly tried.

"We did okay by ourselves last night, didn't we? Even with that imbecile Mr. Zamechnik gumming up the works." Mrs. Mooshman loped over to Gilly's door. "The light is on and the door is open!" she said in a stage whisper. "Doesn't look good!"

"Yes, I know."

"Okay, you ease the door open, and I'll run in and apprehend the pervert," the older woman ordered. She assumed a fighting position and a fierce grimace.

Well, she might not be able to hurt anybody, but

with that face and the rollers, she could sure put the fear of God into them.

Gilly creaked the door open another inch or two. Carefully edging herself into the doorway, she squinted into the apartment. Everything looked normal, everything except...the teenage boy squatting on the floor of the living room, so intent on the paintbrush in his hand he hadn't heard any of the commotion in the hallway.

"Tony," Gilly said, sagging with relief. She waved her mutant ninja neighbor away. "It's okay. It's just my student, the one who's painting my wall."

Mrs. Mooshman didn't wait for an invitation. She swept past Gilly, waving her flashlight like a baton, and advanced on Tony, whose jaw dropped when he saw the older woman's getup. "You should be ashamed, young man, almost giving a nice girl like Gilly a heart attack. We could've brained you by mistake before we knew it was you, because our plan of attack was all ready, wasn't it, Gilly? I'll tell you, Mr. Smarty Pants, we were ready to let a little blood, and that blood would've been yours!"

"I—I'm sorry," he stuttered. "I was only trying to finish. I guess I got kinda caught up in what I was doing."

"Tony, you can't just come over any time you like," Gilly said with considerable heat. "You have to ask first, you know."

"Sorry." He let his paintbrush drop, fixing her with woeful puppy-dog eyes. "I'm so close to being done, though. I didn't hurt anything, Ms. Q. I figured you'd be home and you'd let me in. But you weren't here. So I just kinda came in and went ahead. I didn't think it was a big deal."

"You didn't think at all. And how exactly did you get in?" she asked, not terribly sure she wanted to know.

"The fire escape. You really ought to get that window fixed, Ms. Q," he said helpfully, "because the latch is broken and anybody could come right in."

"Anybody did."

"But I'm like family, Ms. Q. Aren't I?"

She gave him a dirty look. "Kind of." It was the Benedict Academy motto—*We're more than just a school. We're family.* But that was hardly relevant at this moment. "Tony, even if you were my real live blood-is-thicker-than-water brother, I'd still be furious." She crossed her arms over her chest. "You'd better get your brushes and paints cleaned up and get out of here. I haven't decided what I'm going to do with you yet, but for tonight, you're going home immediately. Your mother is probably frantic. I'd better give her a call."

"She ain't home," he said sulkily. "She got a night job."

"So who stays with you?"

"Nobody." The sulk intensified. "I'm thirteen, man. I don't need no baby-sitter."

"Yeah, okay, big boy. Well, you're in trouble, anyway. And I'll talk to your mom first thing tomorrow." Gilly turned to her neighbor. "Mr. Zamechnik still has a car, right? Maybe he could drive Tony home."

"Hah! The imbecile's blind as a bat," Mrs. Mooshman retorted. "I should better accompany them to make sure they get there in one piece." And she trotted off on her mission—supposedly to round up Mr. Zamechnik and his car, but really to launch round 159 in her ongoing battle of words with her favorite sparring partner.

"Tony, I appreciate the beautiful job you're doing on the mural, but that doesn't excuse breaking into my apartment," Gilly said severely, prodding him into cleaning up his supplies. "I'll still pay you—you did the work, so you get paid—but what you did tonight wasn't good. Not good at all."

Still, after she'd gotten him settled in Mr. Zamechnik's car and had retreated back to the safety of her own place, Gilly paced the living room, thanking her lucky stars it had only been Tony.

She frowned, pushing aside her curtain far enough to stare out into the night. Up above her on the bluff she could almost make out the high spires of Blackthorn Manor, rising like a castle in the night.

She rubbed her arms. Nothing had happened. Nothing at all. So why couldn't she shake this feeling that something was very wrong out there in the world?

And whatever it was, it had her name written all over it.

Chapter Five

Things seemed a lot brighter with the start of a new day. Gilly was back to singing about sunshine and blue skies as she took off for school. She had almost convinced herself that last night's fears were the result of an overactive imagination when she turned the corner from Beech onto Marlowe, and that tingly creepy sensation started all over again.

"Probably Marlowe Street's equivalent of Mrs. Mooshman has her eyes peeled for good gossip," Gilly told herself sternly, casting an uneasy glance around the street. "Or maybe some member of the NOD Squad's keeping watch."

But it didn't feel like that, and she didn't see any senior citizens peeking out from behind their curtains. No, it felt like she was being spied on. And she didn't like it one bit.

At least she recognized plenty of people on the street this morning—Benedict Academy students, a friend from one of the neighborhood committees she was on and a cop on the beat. In that environment it was hard to feel nervous about a pair of unknown watching eyes.

But she did.

This was so unlike her. Everyone knew she was take-charge, never-say-die Gillian Quinn. Afraid of a shadow man? Hah!

So why was the hair on the back of her neck standing up? And why did this brilliant winter morning seem chilly and dismal all of a sudden?

With a shiver she ran up the stairs into the academy, determined to put this silliness behind her and get on with her day. She had five classes and two committee meetings, plus that darned press release she still hadn't gotten around to, not to mention a field trip to the art museum later that evening. Oh, and she had to call Tony's mother about last night. She didn't have time for groundless fears.

"Excuse me, Miss Quinn, but could I speak to you a moment, please?" Lena Winslow, the Latin teacher, was wearing one of her perennial pained expressions. There were permanent wrinkles etched in the poor woman's forehead from so much worry. "I'm in charge of Career Day, but of course you know that."

"Of course." Miss Winslow was *always* in charge of Career Day.

"Mrs. Dayton, the assistant principal, suggested that you might be able to deliver Lucas Blackthorn, the photographer, for one of my panels." Her usual frown twisted into a sort of hopeful grimace. "Should I pencil him in?"

"I think I remember mentioning Career Day, and he said he would think about it." She'd definitely asked him to fund a scholarship, and if she could use his name on flyers. Had she worked Career Day in there, too? "I don't remember for sure, though. Why don't I check with him and get back to you?"

"Excellent," Miss Winslow breathed. "I need the

final approval by the end of next week. So don't delay—get that okay today.''

The Latin teacher looked positively merry as she wandered back to her classroom. Gilly mentally added one more item to her list of things that had to be done today.

Luckily the kids in her first class were doing very well with *Twelfth Night,* so she could leave them reading act 3 at the end of the period and dash back to her office cubicle. She hastily put in a call to Tony's mother, who wasn't home. Next on the list—Luke.

The phone was answered on the first ring. ''Yes?'' Aunt Abby whispered.

''Still keeping the noise down, hmm?''

''Hello, Gillian.'' Before Gilly had even had a chance to ask, her aunt said, ''No, you may not speak to Lucas. He's resting.''

''I won't disturb him, I promise. It'll be a very quick phone call.''

''No.'' And the phone clicked in Gilly's ear.

She just sat there, staring at the receiver. Her aunt had hung up on her! What in the world—

The bell rang for second period, so she had no opportunity to dwell on this uncharacteristic rude behavior. Instead, she started the fourth graders' decoupage Valentine's Day projects, thinking about Aunt Abby while she brought out the glue pots and the construction paper.

She found herself so distracted that she finally asked the teacher's aide from the room next door to come over and supervise just this once so she could sneak back and try the phone again.

Again the phone only rang once before Aunt Abigail answered. ''Now don't hang up,'' Gilly said hurriedly, "until you give me an explanation. I can't believe you of all people would hang up without saying goodbye. It's positively medieval!"

"They didn't have phones in medieval times," Abby said crisply. "As a teacher, you should know that."

"Why are you angry with me? I didn't do anything." At least, not as far as she knew. "What is this all about?"

Her aunt didn't answer directly. "Stop harassing Luke," she hissed as if that said it all.

"Harassing?" Gilly was stung. "A person pays a visit out of concern and friendship, and this is construed as harassment?"

"If you had your way," her aunt said angrily, "Lucas would be gallivanting around like a schoolboy. I would think after your misbehavior Wednesday night and the state he was in afterward, you would give up and let the poor boy rest in peace."

Wednesday? But that was the night of the city-council meeting, after which she'd stopped by and...kissed him. Her cheeks flamed with heat. "He told you about that? It was an accident." She muttered, "I can't believe he told you."

"You've hurt him badly, Gillian, and I will not allow you to hurt him again. He's just not strong enough for your kind of roughhousing. Now leave him alone!" And Aunt Abigail cut the connection again.

So much for family ties.

Gilly felt as if Aunt Abby had slapped her in the face. "But I didn't do anything wrong," she protested. The only one listening was that stupid newspaper photo of Luke tacked to her cubicle wall.

Feeling quite mistreated and misunderstood, Gilly

backtracked to the art class in time to help the students finish their Valentine's boxes, and then slid into automatic pilot to cover a section of *Canterbury Tales* with her sixth graders. After that, it was eighth-grade drama, with students who were bouncing off the walls, and finally, finally, she had her lunch break.

Calming herself, she tried Tony's mother again and had a nice chat about what a good boy he was and how hard Mrs. Fielder was trying to keep tabs on him. Then she drafted the long-awaited press release and asked the school secretary to type it up and send it out. Normally she wouldn't have dumped that on someone else, but she just didn't have time.

As she worked, Luke and Aunt Abby stayed in the back of her mind. Had Luke really told her aunt about the kiss? As if it were some sort of juvenile stunt she'd pulled to irritate him?

The longer she thought about it, the madder she got. At Aunt Abby, sure, but also at infuriating, touch-me-not Luke. She couldn't recall ever being this angry at him. Certainly, he annoyed her sometimes, but she always forgave him, feeling that their friendship was worth a little inconvenience. But not this time. She was in no mood to forgive him for telling her aunt about that poor innocent kiss.

So she waited until just after one, when she felt sure Aunt Abigail would be out doing her shopping and unable to play phone-interference games. And then she called him again, punching in the numbers with as much force as she could get into one finger.

It rang twice. A good sign.

"Hello?"

"Uncle Fitz," she said with relief. "I'm so glad I got you. Can I please talk to Luke?"

"No, I'm sorry, Gilly." His voice was like ice. "After the last time you saw him, he has been most unwell. Your aunt and I have decided it is not in his best interests to be under your influence right now."

"Under my influence?" Had everyone at Blackthorn Manor lost their minds? "I'm hardly going to influence him with one simple phone call! Come on, Uncle Fitz, put him on the phone."

Uncle Fitz remained implacable. "No. When you talk to him, you convince him to undertake dangerous activities."

"What are you talking about? Dangerous activities?" she repeated. "Let's see... I asked him to have dinner with me. I asked him to contribute money to the Benedict Academy. Oh, and I guess I also asked him to speak at Career Day and maybe come to the Snow Ball. Gee whiz, that's a real dangerous lineup, isn't it?"

There was silence on the other end of the phone.

So she tried a different tack. "Fizzy, this is Gilly you're talking to. You and I both know that Luke is a very strong and capable person. It won't hurt him in the least to come to the St. Benny's career fair. And he already agreed to help with the anti-casino campaign and a scholarship fund. He can't back out now."

She wished she could remember her conversation with Luke a bit better, but then she'd accidentally kissed him, and *then* she'd held off two knife-toting muggers with a trash-can lid and been saved by a phantom in a dark alley, so she felt she could be forgiven for forgetting a few details. That had been a rough night.

"Gillian," her uncle said softly, "you must understand that your problems at the Benedict Academy are not as important right now as Luke's getting a chance to recuperate.''

Not as important? Not as important? St. Benny's was in danger of being leveled by bulldozers at any moment, and its problems weren't as important as Luke's taking a nap?

She could've spit.

"Look, I don't know why you guys are so sure talking to me is such a perilous activity,'' she returned hotly. "But you're all wet, okay? I'm the best thing that could happen to him, because I represent the real world, instead of Blackthorn Manor, the fairy castle. Tell Luke I will talk to him. Soon.''

And this time *she* hung up.

Steaming, she resolved that Luke was not getting off the hook that easily, no matter how mean her aunt and uncle got. She needed Luke, damn it. He had the money, the clout and the hero status that could really make a difference. Forget what he wanted. She needed him, and she *would* make him an integral part of her mission to save St. Benny's.

"He's the only one who can help,'' she declared, throwing a pencil at his smug face. "And he's going to help, whether he likes it or not.''

"KIDS, STAY TOGETHER, please,'' Gilly commanded. Normally she would've loved chaperoning the honors arts students when they visited the museum, especially since both Tony and another child had pictures in the student art fair. Goodness knew, she should've been able to handle a mere ten kids by herself.

But today was just one of those days.

"Susie, stay with the group, please!'' she called as the pretty little brunette wandered away to look at some Egyptian antiquities. "Come on back. We're going the other way to find the gallery with Tony and Amanda's pictures."

Reluctantly Susie hopped back into formation, and their ragtag group forged on.

If the kids had been a little younger, Gilly could've tied them together and carried the reins herself. Too bad that choice was no longer available. "Kendall, Caleb—back with the group, please."

After bouncing through a series of rooms labeled Treasures of the Ancient World, they finally made it to the big open gallery where the student exhibit was. The gallery was filled to the brim with teens and preteens, probably a good sign that they were in the right place.

"Stay together," Gilly tried one last time, but the presence of so many cute members of the opposite sex was like honey to a hive of bees. Gilly left the students to their socializing while she dutifully admired the artwork. And then she hung around until she could reasonably collect her charges and shoo them back into the minibus.

As she idled, she noticed that Susie had sneaked back to the Treasures of the Ancient World. Better go after her, she decided, before the girl got any further afield.

"Wow, Ms. Q, did you see this?" Susie asked, her voice hushed with awe, her nose pressed to a glass case. "There are vases and pottery and this really cool painting where the lady doesn't have a top on and she's carrying snakes. It's so cool!"

Minoan Snake Priestess, Gilly read off the card. "It is interesting, isn't it?"

"I just love this ancient stuff," Susie said with a

sigh. "I did like the Greeks the best, but now I think these Minoans are just too cool. There are snakes and bulls everywhere. Does that mean something—snakes and bulls?"

"I don't know a whole lot about the Minoans, but if you want to do some research and do a special project when we get back to school, I think that would be great."

"Cool!"

"But right now we really need to round up the rest of the gang." Gilly glanced at her watch. "It's past time to get back."

"Bummer." But the girl came along willingly enough. And then it was a game of hide-and-seek for several minutes until everybody was tracked down and accounted for, then finally herded back onto the bus.

Gilly sank into her seat, ready to rest for a minute.

But then Javier, one of her savvier students, asked, "Ms. Quinn, who was that guy following you?"

Her blood chilled. "What guy?" she asked carefully.

"Didn't you see him? Wherever we went, he went," Javier told her. "I thought maybe it was Tony's dad 'cause, you know, sometimes Tony has to look out for him, but this guy was white."

"What did he look like?"

"Tall, I guess. Kinda old, like at least as old as you. I don't know." He lifted his narrow shoulders. "Hard to tell, y'know."

"Yeah, I know." She swallowed. "No, I didn't see him, Javier. Why did you think he was following me?"

"At first I wasn't sure, because it could've just been a coincidence, like he wanted to look at the same things we did." The boy's face furrowed with concentration. "But then when you went to get Susie, he went there, too. And that seemed weird to me."

"You did the right thing by telling me," she assured him. "Good job, Javier."

So she *was* being followed, and that creepy feeling wasn't just her imagination. Whoever this jerk was, he was following when her students were around, which was even worse. But who would follow *her*?

She hadn't come up with any real suspects by the time the bus dropped them all off at her apartment, where the field trip entered phase two. She'd had this brilliant idea to treat them all to a picnic supper at her place and show off her new living-room mural as the perfect end to their art-centered trip.

Now she just wished she could take a hot bath and be alone for a few minutes. She shook her head as she opened the door and let the kids in. This, too, was unlike her. She was indefatigable; didn't everyone always say that?

But that was before Luke came back into her life, making her angry and frustrated, before muggers decided to come after her with knives, before Nightshade and his groupies haunted her at every turn, before some maniac started following her night and day.

Now she was tired and cranky and antisocial. Oh, God. She was turning into Luke.

The kids were rambunctious and hungry, so she turned on some music for them as she made hot dogs and dished out chips and soft drinks. It literally took ten minutes to throw their supper together. They were all laughing and running around the small apartment, having a great time, creating quite a ruckus what with both the TV and the CD player blaring. Gilly didn't even hear the phone when it rang.

"Ms. Quinn, it's the telephone!" one of her students called out over the din, holding up the receiver. "It's for you!"

She skirted a path through kids and hot dogs and flying potato chips, finally arriving at the phone. Covering her free ear, she shouted, "Hello?" into the receiver.

"It's Luke," he said tersely. "Please don't shout at me. And what the hell is going on over there?"

"Luke?" This was a surprise. After the reception she'd gotten from her aunt and uncle, she really hadn't expected to hear from him. "Could you speak up? I can hardly hear you."

"Are you having a party?"

"No," she told him, still talking loudly just to hear herself over the commotion in her apartment. "Just some of my art students."

"I thought artists might've been a quieter bunch."

He sounded marginally more amused than pained, so she let it pass. But she steeled herself to retain her anger and not let him get to her the way he always did.

"Hold on a sec," she said, carrying the cordless phone into her bedroom where it was a lot calmer and giving herself a chance to concentrate on being mad at him. "Okay, now I'm away from the hubbub. Talk."

"I hear you were so anxious to talk to me that you threatened both Fitzhughs with bodily harm," he told her dryly. "A matter of life and death. And then you run off and have a party?"

"I didn't threaten anyone with anything, much as I

would've liked to," she returned tartly. "Did you know that dear Aunt Abigail took me to task for corrupting your morals?"

"What?" Even Luke's soft voice rose on that one.

Well, perhaps she shouldn't have said that part about corrupting his morals. That wasn't exactly what Aunt Abby had said. Still, that was the implication. Without thinking, she said hotly, "You told her about the kiss! How could you?"

Oh, well. She had hoped to live her life without ever mentioning the damn thing, but her tongue sort of got away from her.

"I did what?" he demanded.

"The kiss, stupid! You told her about that innocent, unplanned little accident in the kitchen. So then she accused me of hurting you, as if I were the town bad girl leading you on or something." She paused for a breath. "Lucas Blackthorn, brokenhearted over one kiss? I hardly think so! I told her *and* Uncle Fitz that you were not the type—"

"But I didn't," he interrupted.

"Didn't what?"

"I didn't say anything to Abigail about the—" He broke off suddenly, and his voice dropped even lower. "About the kiss. Why would I tell my housekeeper?"

"Well, I couldn't imagine why you would." Somewhat mollified, Gilly shook her head. Thank goodness. At least he'd had the sense not to spill the beans to Abby. "She knows, though. She called it my 'misbehavior on Wednesday.' What else could it be?"

Silence greeted her over the telephone wire.

"What else could it be?" she asked again.

"I don't know," he said finally in an odd, strained voice.

"I suppose she could just mean visiting you so late, talking you into helping St. Benny's, that kind of thing," she said doubtfully. "Did you tell her about that?"

"No."

"Oh. But you're still going to help, aren't you?" She moved closer to the bedroom window, where she could gaze up at the bluff where his house stood. "You promised, Luke."

His voice was terse and cool when he responded. "I'll tell Abigail to cut a check for your fund tomorrow. How much do you want?"

"It costs about three thousand dollars a year for each of our students' tuition. You could sponsor a student—or a couple—if you wanted to."

"Fine."

"Are you in a hurry or something? You sound awfully abrupt," she said thoughtfully.

"Sorry. I didn't mean to be." He hesitated, and his tone became a tad darker, more dangerous. "I'm just furious that my household servants have taken it upon themselves to censor my phone calls and interfere in my personal life. It's obscene."

"So you didn't tell them to turn me away, no matter the cost?"

His voice softened. "No, of course not."

Oh, heavens. When he sounded like that, she could forgive him just about anything. She sent a hopeful glance up at Blackthorn Manor, imagining Luke in his rumpled clothes, maybe lying on his bed as he cradled the phone. The image was irresistible. But if she asked him what he was wearing, it would sound like some sleazy 900 line. She refrained, steering herself back to business.

"Luke, I already sent out the press release with your name on it. It says we're organizing a campaign to save the neighborhood, and as an alum of St. Benny's you're standing with us. You okayed that, right?"

His tone was rueful. "I suppose this means the press is going to be down on me big-time now that they know where I am."

"Maybe." She hesitated, chewing her lip. "I didn't say where you were, but I suppose they could figure it out. But I couldn't wait! We only have two weeks till the city council votes. And without someone with some clout on our team, it's down the tubes for St. Benny's."

"Just Benny's. Not a saint anymore, remember?"

"Yeah, I know. It's a hard habit to break." She sat on the edge of the bed, but she could still see through the window, up to the outline of his mansion against the winter sky. "It's not just St. Benny's—I mean, Benny's—that'll go under the wrecking ball, you know. My apartment building is safe for the time being, but half my students' homes, my parents' old house on Division Street—they're all scheduled to go. Even the museum where I took my students on a field trip today won't be saved. You'd love the museum, Luke. They have a photography gallery that may even have some of your stuff in it. And a great collection of things from ancient Greece and Minoa."

"There is no Minoa," he corrected. "Minoans were from Crete."

She sat up straighter. "Like your cave?"

"Exactly like my cave," he returned.

"Well, you might want to check out the Minoan collection, then. You might be very interested in the paintings and the pottery, because they probably look like your photo of that cow." She was being devious, but she couldn't help it. "Of course, you'd better go as soon as possible. Because that museum will be ancient history itself if the city council has its way."

"Oh, Gilly, what am I going to do with you?" But she could hear the amusement in his voice. "I said I would help, didn't I?"

"So I can put you down on my committee?" she said eagerly. "You'd be a real presence at Benny's, on our side all the way. So you'll come to Career Day, right? And the Snow Ball?"

"Wait a minute. I never said—" He stopped and started again, more resolute this time. "I can't, Gilly. Money is no problem and I'll allow you to use my name any way you see fit. But my name, not my body. I can't leave the house yet. Not yet."

"But, Luke—"

"Abigail will send you a check first thing in the morning." His voice was so soft she had to strain to hear it. "That's the best I can do."

"Let's at least talk about this," she tried. "What about the museum? I could meet you there and show you—"

But he had already hung up.

"The people at that house are so rude," she told the receiver.

She knew she had already spent too much time away from the children in her living room and she had to get back. But if she hadn't been otherwise occupied, she swore she would've marched right up to the manor and given Luke a piece of her mind.

What was he so afraid of? Why did he insist he couldn't leave the house? This was globe-trotting, thrill-seeking Lucas Blackthorn they were talking about. It was all just too weird for her.

"Okay, kids, party's over," she announced, falling back into instructor mode as she reentered the living room. She'd left them alone a good ten minutes and nothing was destroyed. What a turn of events! "Susie, you're riding with Amanda, right? Kendall, your mother is at the door."

But once she had them cleaned up and sent off with the right number of parents and rides, her apartment seemed awfully quiet.

As the shadows deepened in West Riverside, as evening passed into night, Gilly was still brooding about Luke.

"Damn him, anyway!" Didn't he know how much she needed his face at a few rallies? Didn't he know how much good it could do for a high-and-mighty Blackthorn like him to pay a visit or two to a well-placed politico? Luke was a hero. And she needed him on her side.

But it didn't look like she was going to get him.

"You know, Luke," she announced to the dark window, "if you won't come out of that place and help me, I really have only one choice."

She paused, giving the towers of Blackthorn Manor an appraising look.

"Back to plan A." She smiled. "I storm the citadel."

Chapter Six

Gilly marched out of her apartment, ready to go forth and do battle. But she hadn't stepped one foot away from her door when she heard screams.

"Stop, thief!" Mrs. Mooshman cried, flapping the door to the stairs as she struggled to hold on to someone just inside the stairwell.

Gilly ran to her side. It was all very confusing, but there appeared to be a rather small, disheveled man in there, and he was desperately trying to shake himself loose from Mrs. Mooshman's ferocious grasp.

"I've got him!" Mrs. Mooshman yelled triumphantly, wrapping his arm in a death grip and trying to smack him with her flashlight with her free hand. "Let go of my mother's candlesticks," she puffed, giving him a few good whacks and trying with all her might to drag him into the hall.

Dropping her backpack, Gilly propped open the door with one foot and maneuvered around to get a good grip of her own on the guy. He had a knit mask over his face and he smelled awful. He had quite a mouth on him, too. He cursed the women in two different languages as they struggled. But he was fairly small, and the two of them together were making progress, inching him out of the stairwell. At last they managed to tug the top half of him into the hall and knock him down, and then Gilly sat on his chest to hold him. With a fearsome scream, Mrs. Mooshman wound up and clonked him on the head with the flashlight. The bandit went limp.

"Let's get him into the hall here," Mrs. Mooshman suggested. She was out of breath, but she went on, anyway, dragging and talking at the same time. "I suppose I'll have to go into his pockets if I want my money. Dirty, filthy creep! He broke into my apartment, do you believe it? There I was, watching 'The Gossip Show' in my bedroom, and I heard my front door open. So I got my flashlight, and there he was, the creep, big as life, stealing my mother's good silver candlesticks and taking all my cash out of that little box I keep on the mantel. He even took my NOD whistle and my Dresden shepherdess! Well, I got him, didn't I?" The old lady kicked him with one house slipper.

"Mrs. Mooshman, he could've had a gun," Gilly protested. "You shouldn't have run after him yourself."

"Oh, fiddle-faddle." But as her neighbor bent over to retrieve her beloved candlesticks, the burglar suddenly reared up, taking them both by surprise. With a snarl, he pushed Mrs. Mooshman to her knees, grabbed the candlesticks and brandished one high in the air, threatening to bash Gilly's head in.

With one final rush of motion, he seized Gilly's backpack and began to scuttle down the stairs with his booty.

"Call the police!" Gilly cried, scuttling right after him. No way some scumbag was stealing her backpack, loaded down with money and ID, a bunch of school stuff—even her sixth graders' corrected French papers. "Drop it, buster!"

He might've been small, but he was pretty fast, and he was down the stairs and out into the street a few strides ahead of her.

On the straightaway, her long legs and his heavy burdens began to make a difference. She was catching up. If she could just bridge those final inches, she felt sure she could snag the strap of her backpack.

But her lungs felt like they were going to explode from gulping in too much of the icy air, and her sturdy boots were having trouble finding purchase on the slippery ice and snow. Even the streetlights were conspiring against her; most of them seemed to be burned out or broken.

Dark. Cold. Slippery. But she had to catch him. She had to.

Just out of reach. So close. Not quite yet. *Now.*

Putting everything she had into one final burst of energy, she lunged for the thief. But her fingers curled around nothing but air. And her face contacted neither his smelly body nor the hard cold ground.

Instead, she was dangling in the wind, captured in midleap. Hard solid arms held her fast.

Astonished, she cried, "He's getting away!" and wriggled and tussled against the binding embrace. But the grip only tightened. And then she took a good look at who exactly held her so securely.

There was no helpful streetlight to illuminate him, but it didn't matter. Identifying the dark stranger was a cinch. "Nightshade," she whispered.

Of course it was him. Who else was that tall, that intense, shrouded in a long black coat and a fedora, with a soft inky scarf obscuring his jaw? Oh, yes, and he was wearing a pair of impenetrable black sunglasses.

"Nightshade," she said again, and her body seemed to tingle and burn where his gloved hands held her. "Where did you come from?"

"I heard you scream for help," he whispered.

"But how? I was completely alone—"

He put a gloved finger, soft and warm, over her lips. "It doesn't matter. Just know that when you're in trouble, I will hear you."

She was close enough to feel the energy and heat that radiated from him, and to know without a doubt that he was strong, lean, powerfully built. His thick dark coat might conceal his body from her eyes, but not from her fingers. As she reached for him, he hauled her into his arms completely, toting her to an even darker corner.

"Stay here," he growled.

"What?" She had been so dazzled by the strange power that seemed to emanate from Nightshade that she had almost forgotten the goon who'd stolen her backpack. "Oh, the thief!" she said suddenly. "I have to go after him! He stole—"

"Stay put!"

"But I—"

The man they called Nightshade simply pulled her into his arms and kissed her, branding her fiercely with the heat and force of his lips.

Oh, God. She had never felt anything like it. Summer bonfires, hot-fudge sundaes, zero gravity... Her mind was whirling, and her body seemed to have dissolved into a puddle of pure bliss. If she thought the kiss she had given Luke was intense, it was nothing compared to this. It was like turning up the oven so far the knob broke off in your hand, and then you just roasted in the unchecked flames.

She gave in, melting, breathless, tingling, but too soon he set her away from him. And then he left!

Gilly was still reeling as he took off in hot pursuit of the creep. Through the haze that clouded her brain, she watched him dash down the street, ducking into the shadows and abandoning the light.

"He'll catch him," she murmured.

And he did.

She was still staring down the street in the direction he'd disappeared when he grabbed her from behind, scaring the living daylights out of her. Without a word, he pulled two candlesticks, the backpack, a small porcelain figurine and a wad of money out from the far reaches of his coat, dumping it all into her arms.

"Your perp is stinking up an alley off Poplar Street," he rasped, his low gruff voice sounding for all the world like Clint Eastwood's. "He's not moving."

And then he kissed her again, quickly, before disappearing into the shadows with his long black coat swirling out behind him.

"I don't know who he is," Gilly said slowly, "but I sure wish I did."

Juggling the loot, she raised a shaky finger to her lips. She could still feel the fiery imprint of his lips on hers. She shivered. She could also still feel the pressure of his gloved fingers on her arms.

She felt as if she'd been made love to, thoroughly and completely, when all he'd done was kiss her into mind-numbing ecstasy. She felt as if she'd finally met the man of her dreams.

Of course, she didn't know what his name was or even what he looked like. But those were mere details.

He'd kissed her. It was incredible. *He* was incredible.

But who *was* he?

"Hey, Gillian Quinn!" a strident voice called out. "I've got three eyewitnesses who say Nightshade was just here. What can you tell me?"

Devon Drake was moving pretty quickly this time. Blinking, Gilly refocused on reality as the wily blonde came jogging up, her notebook and recorder at the ready.

"He went that way," Gilly announced lightly, pointing down a particularly ugly alley in the opposite direction from the path Nightshade had taken. An odd sort of joy was bubbling below the surface of her consciousness, and she had to hold back a smile. "Maybe you can catch him."

"In these heels? Don't be ridiculous." Devon pursed her heavily glossed lips. "I'm never going to catch Nightshade in a footrace. No, I'm going to catch him with terrific reporting." She smiled deviously. "This is going to work great with a story I was already working on for tomorrow. Crime on the rise in West Riverside, mayor calling for cleanup—all the usual stuff. But now Nightshade foiling a burglary attempt, well, that takes it to a whole new level, doesn't it?"

"You're going to use this to bash West Riverside one more time?" Gilly groaned. "Come on—can't you find a different angle?"

But Devon Drake just shook her head. "It fits too neatly, hon. I'd be crazy not to use it. And then..." Her eyes lit up. "I'm going to get a sketch artist to do a composite. I'm going to publish every description

I can find. I've already got a psychologist working on a profile. Because when I'm done Nightshade won't have any more secrets from me—including his identity.''

"This isn't a super-hero comic book," Gilly reminded the reporter.

But Devon was racing ahead. "What can you tell me, Ms. Quinn? Oh, and don't leave anything out," she ordered, her pen poised over her notebook.

I've never seen his face, but I know he's gorgeous. I've never had a conversation with him, but I know he's honest and brave and kind. Instead of that lovestruck nonsense, Gilly reeled off the usual list. "He's tall, he's Caucasian, and he wears a black coat, sunglasses and the kind of hat Humphrey Bogart used to wear in the old movies. Try *Casablanca*," she put in helpfully. "Other than that...I can't think of a thing."

"Height? Weight? Hair color? Eye color?"

"I don't know, I don't know, I don't know and I don't know." Gilly smiled sweetly. "But hey, listen, good luck! I really have to go." She lifted her arms, indicating the pile of items Nightshade had dropped there. "I need to return my neighbor's belongings. I'm sure you'll excuse me."

As Devon scrambled to interview the other witnesses, Gilly walked home in a daze. *He kissed me.*

"Wow," kept rolling off her lips. "Wow."

She might've called him dreamy if it didn't sound so much like a high-school crush. But dreamy he was.

The police were talking to Mrs. Mooshman when Gilly got upstairs. She cheerfully relayed the information about where Nightshade had left the culprit, wordlessly turned over the candlesticks, the shepherdess and the money, then drifted to her own door.

"Gilly, what's wrong with you?" her neighbor demanded. "Did the burglar hit you over the head or something? You're acting all moony and weird all of a sudden."

"No." She offered a distracted smile. "I'm fine." *I've been kissed by a mysterious stranger and I'll never be the same again. But I'm fine.*

"You might be in shock, ma'am," the policeman noted. "You should probably go to the hospital and get checked over."

"I'm fine," she said again. "G'night, Mrs. M."

"Hey, you didn't bring back my whistle," Mrs. Mooshman exclaimed in disappointment.

Gilly paid no attention. She was practically dancing into her apartment, locking and double-bolting the door.

"I've been kissed by a mysterious stranger and I'll never be the same again," she said with a laugh as she waltzed into a nightgown and climbed into bed. "But I am *so* fine!"

GILLY DREAMED she was dancing in the dark. "Ahhh," she murmured, sinking deeper into the heavenly dream.

She was wearing a diaphanous white dress, kind of like the girl in the Bible with the seven veils. Her red hair was longer, less curly, more wavy and flowing, and her skin was very, very pale, almost as white as the filmy dress.

She knew her dress hid nothing, that every inch of her was visible and that her nipples pressed against the transparent fabric, impudent and blatant, and she knew she was very wicked to be flaunting her charms this way.

But the knowledge only made her more brazen. She sent peals of joyous laughter to join the stars and the moon. Practically naked, dancing like a hoyden, she felt happy and alive, enchanted and enchanting.

Because *he* was watching.

He hovered in the shadows, wordless, but watchful. She could see the long dark silhouette he cast. She knew exactly where he stood, where he waited.

The moon glistened on her bare shoulders, casting opalescent sparkles on her hands and her cheeks. There were paving stones under her bare feet, and she whirled and twirled, feeling the silken fabric float around her ankles, drift over her calves, caress her thighs.

It was delicious.

She felt beautiful and untamed, and she knew he followed every tiny movement. She felt a surge of power, her own power over the man in the shadows, and a rush of moon-drenched desire that soaked her to the bone. It made her dance faster, more wildly, crazily, until she knew he must stop.

But she couldn't stop. Spinning and twisting, she was growing tired and disoriented, but still she could not rest. It was as if he commanded the dance, and only at his pleasure could she find relief from the feverish pace.

And then, just at the moment she thought she would drop of exhaustion, when she could not go one more step, his arms caught her, held her, swept her up in his embrace.

The dance continued. But now it was different. Very different.

He was all darkness and danger; he smelled of nighttime, of midnight, of slashing rain and angry storms. But she curled into him, pressing her face into his wet black collar, brushing his neck and his jaw with her hungry lips. He, too, pressed hot kisses into the pale cool gauze of her dress, driving her mad.

"Who are you?" she cried. Even from the depths of her desire, she knew she must know his name.

But he did not answer. Instead, he continued to stroke her and touch her, until she could barely breathe with the heady passion sliding through her veins.

"No, no," she whimpered. "I must know who you are."

She cupped his face with her hands and looked deep into his eyes. But even so close, she couldn't make out his features. It was as if a mist had passed before her eyes, and she could not quite break through it.

He pressed her down onto the rough paving stones, his clever hands stoking the fires higher, until she clung to him, hanging on for dear life, letting the waves of fire carry her away.

She whispered, "Make love to me. Now. I want to feel you inside me. I love you, Nightshade. I've always loved you...."

"LUKE!"

She awoke with a start, feeling very strange. Her body was tingling and flushed, and the bed clothes were all rumpled.

What in the world had she been dreaming about?

Gilly blinked. She put a hand to her head, still woozy. She had some vague memory of the dream, but it was very hazy, something about dancing under the moon in hardly any clothing.

Well, that was different. Usually her dreams were

more like nightmares, in which she was frantically trying to teach her class as all her teeth fell out.

But dancing naked was a whole new experience.

"Nightshade," she whispered. "Nightshade was there. So I was dancing naked with Nightshade. Oh, my God."

As she fell back into the pillows, she felt hot shame suffuse her. As fair-skinned as she was, she could blush from head to toe. And she was doing a pretty good job of it right now.

"I'm not this sort of person," she wailed, wanting these feelings to go away. Far, far away. *Now.* "Just because I haven't made love in the nineties is no reason to send me erotic dreams about a guy whose face I've never seen!"

She swallowed. That was part of the dream, too, wasn't it? Trying to see his face. And not succeeding.

"This is too spooky for me," she murmured, rubbing her arms and shivering under the covers. Try as she might, she couldn't put any other pieces of the dream back together. Dancing naked with Nightshade and trying to see his face was as good as it got. Which wasn't very good.

It was still dark outside, but she knew she would never get back to sleep when she was this restless. Besides, she always wished there were a few more hours in the day. Looked like this was one day she had them. So she swung out of bed and headed for the shower.

It was only when the first rush of water hit her head that she remembered.

"Luke. Something about Luke. But what?"

But whatever it was, it had left her. Grumbling, she finished up and poked her way through her normal morning routine. Why was she so sluggish this morning? And why did she feel like she'd run a marathon somewhere between the time she went to bed and the time she got up?

She was dawdling over the newspaper, cursing Devon Drake and her mean-spirited article about West Riverside, when she saw the much-vaunted sketch of the mysterious Nightshade. She laughed out loud.

"He looks like the Unabomber in a cowboy hat!" she crowed. It was the wrong hat and the total wrong look. So much for Ms. Drake's eyewitnesses.

Just for fun, she read the psychological profile, too. "'A solitary individual, probably not married or living with anyone who might notice his nocturnal disappearances.' Well, that makes sense." She skipped ahead. "'Excellent cognitive skills...high threshold of justice. Maybe someone burned by the system in some way.' Oh, they always say that. 'Probably lives in or near West Riverside, although he may simply have some emotional attachment to the area of which we are unaware.'"

There was certainly nothing there that would help anyone find him. She did like the last line, though. "The fact that this man only appears at night is very significant. He is clearly more comfortable with darkness than with light."

"Nightshade, you are one fascinating guy," Gilly murmured, staring at the awful sketch.

And then she spied the date at the top of the page.

"Oh, no," she moaned. "The one day I'm up early and it's Saturday. A completely free, unencumbered Saturday when I could've slept till noon! Way to go— kill my only day to sleep late, Nightshade!"

Determined to rediscover the joys of a warm bed,

Gilly dodged back under the covers. Only to find herself sitting straight up some fifteen minutes later.

"Of course I was thinking about Luke. I was on my way to his house when I got sidetracked by Mrs. Mooshman and the burglar."

This time she arose with a sense of purpose, ready once again to storm the citadel.

SHE WAITED until after eleven, when she figured Abby and Fitz would be occupied. She knew their schedule pretty well after all these years. On Saturdays Aunt Abigail liked to have Uncle Fitz drive her to flea markets and swap meets. You'd never know it to look at her, but Aunt Abby had a fondness for knitted toilet-paper covers and mismatched teacups. Even now, with Luke requiring more care than usual, Gilly knew Aunt Abby wouldn't be able to resist a trip to Bargain Heaven.

Still, Gilly knew better than to try the front door. Luke was perfectly capable of simply lurking in there, refusing to answer no matter how hard she pounded.

Instead, she took a page from her childhood escapades and scaled the ivy on the west wall. It made her smile just to grab hold and take the first step up on the vine. As she recalled, this bountiful crop of ivy grew right up to Luke's bedroom. And he had a balcony. Both of those facts had proved very useful when they were sixteen and way past curfew, and Luke had to sneak in before Aunt Abby caught him.

Gilly had only climbed the ivy to prove she could, because Luke teased her mercilessly about being uncoordinated. She'd shown him, scaling the wall faster than he had.

Now, however, she wasn't nearly as graceful—

she'd been a better climber when she was younger and
more limber—and she was huffing and puffing as she
neared the third floor. But eventually she reached
Luke's room. Letting go of frozen fistfuls of brown
vines, she hoisted herself over the wrought-iron railing
and landed on the balcony, ending up flat on her back-
side.

"Ouch!" she exclaimed before she could stop herself. Rubbing her poor bruised derriere, she stood up
and looked around. There was a great view from up
here, especially now that the trees had no leaves to
block the way. Why, you could see the river and most
of West Riverside.

Well, the view was spectacular, but so was the
wind, and Gilly was chilled all the way through. So
she crouched by the heavy French doors looking for
a clever way in.

She pinged a nail against the glass. She'd heard of
double-hung windows, but this was ridiculous. What
was Luke doing with windows as thick as ice blocks?
After several moments of careful examination, she
pulled out a nail file, ready to try to pry open the lock.
But when she touched the handle, the door swung
open immediately. It wasn't even latched.

"So much for breaking in," she said lightly, peeking past the door before sticking a foot inside.

When her foot caused no uproar, she edged in her
whole leg and then the rest of her, cautious as a cat
in a new yard. Although the room was dim, she knew
one thing: it was still Luke's bedroom. And he wasn't
there. Lucky chance on that one. She didn't think he
would still be sleeping at eleven, but given his recent
odd behavior, there was no way to be sure.

She had been prepared to stumble over him right

away, although she preferred to get a chance to look around first.

"Knowledge is power, Lucas Blackthorn," she said aloud. Curious as hell, she scanned the room.

She couldn't really remember what his bedroom looked like when they were kids. White walls, she thought, and the usual bed and a dresser perhaps. With a chuckle, she remembered the days when Luke had had nothing but a mattress on the floor and a stereo system with a huge set of speakers.

Luke had never been fond of decorating his space, even a big, high-ceilinged space like this. She had joked and called this his "bedchamber" once, since that's what it looked like—something out of a Gothic novel.

But the room was a heck of a lot more Gothic now. "Weird," she muttered, examining the heavy velvet drapes around his bed. "Depressing and weird."

Even his sheets were black. There were headphones, the kind that came with very fancy stereo systems, lying at the foot of the bed, but she didn't see anything to plug them into. A sleep mask and a half-open book had been tossed on the floor next to the bed. She picked up the book and flipped it open to the title page. *"Bats, Nature's Night Warriors,"* she read, and then dropped the book immediately. "Eeeuw. I hate bats."

She tiptoed past the huge draped bed, eyeing the dark painting of an orchid on one wall and the African tribal masks on the other.

The only other furniture besides the bed was a strange-looking apparatus along the far wall. It hummed, so she knew it was electric, but what was it? It was entirely too coffinlike for her, and she was reluctant to get close. But curiosity got the better of her and she edged nearer. When she peered through the little window in the side, she saw what looked like water sloshing around.

"Oh, wait," she murmured, trying to remember where she'd seen something like this before. "The front of a tabloid. Michael Jackson. It's a sensory-deprivation tank. What in the world is Luke doing with one of those?"

She wasn't going to find out by standing there gawking at it, so she left it for the time being. But other than the bed and the tank, there was nothing much in the room. No mirror, no lamps, no dresser spilling over with change and watches and tie tacks. Not that she could've seen if there were, given the dismal lighting conditions.

She pulled back the curtain across the French door, flooding the room with harsh wintry light, somewhat distorted by the thick glass, but still welcome.

"Much better," she said with conviction. No wonder he was skulking around like a member of the Adams family, with a room decorated like this.

The only other thing to look at was the closet. "Oooh," she whispered. "I forgot about the secret passageway."

He'd even taken her in there once when she'd begged and begged. You had to tap just right in the back of the closet, and a panel slid away. It led to a mysterious storage room, full of all kinds of old trunks and toys from ancient Blackthorns.

Should she poke? Was she that nosy?

She had her hand on the knob, ready to go exploring, when a very familiar voice stopped her in her tracks.

"Look what I found," Luke said sardonically. "Gilly Quinn. And here I thought I was being invaded by a traveling troupe of elephants."

Chapter Seven

"Oh, come on, I didn't make that much noise," she protested, releasing the doorknob and assuming an air of innocence.

He merely raised an eyebrow, then strode over to the curtains and yanked them back into place across the window, throwing the room once again into shadow. "You can't resist screwing around with my life, can you, Gilly?"

"Luke, come on. A little light can't hurt you."

"Why in God's name I put up with you is beyond me," he muttered.

"Now *that* sounds like the Luke I know and love." She gazed at him, frankly curious. After all the hue and cry from her aunt and uncle about how unwell he was and how devastated he'd been after her "misbehavior" on the previous Wednesday, she wanted to judge for herself how he was faring.

Even in the dim room, she could see that he looked well. He was wearing black jeans that fit like a glove, and a sweatshirt that had faded to a steely gray. His hair was a little ragged—looked like he needed a trim—and he had on thick soft socks. Comfortable, yet perfectly normal, not eccentric in the least.

It was just as she'd thought—no unexpectedly sensual kiss from an old friend was going to play havoc with that tough hide. *Tough but attractive hide,* she amended mentally. She felt the familiar shiver. No question about it—Lucas Blackthorn had plenty of charm in the looks department.

He certainly seemed healthy enough, with more color and less strain than before. She cocked her head to one side, scrutinizing the rigid set of his jaw, the spark of temper in his blue eyes, the thread of tension in his posture. Well, healthy enough physically, anyway. Emotionally, she wasn't so sure.

"Seen enough?" he asked tersely, glowering at her.

She smiled. "I guess. You look full of vim and vigor. You must be feeling better."

"Actually, I am better," he allowed. "Not perfect, but better able to control, uh, things."

"You always were big on control." Gilly wandered casually toward the big black tank with its faint buzzing sound. She tapped it gently. "And is the sensory-deprivation tank helping?"

For the first time she could remember, Luke seemed taken aback. "I didn't think you'd know what it was."

"Michael Jackson," she said offhandedly. "The tabloids."

There was that eyebrow again.

"Hey, my students bring them to school all the time. I just confiscate them. I don't read them."

"That's what they all say." He paused. "But yes, actually, it is helping," he said finally. He shoved his hands into his pockets, his eyes never leaving her. "It's no big deal. It just helps me relax."

"Sort of re-creating the cave experience?"

"Nothing like the cave experience." His tone was

flat, and he turned and left the bedroom. Whether or not he expected her to follow was anyone's guess.

"Hey, wait up," she called after a last look around. If there were clues to his behavior in the bedroom, she hadn't found any. Except that his room seemed more like a cave than a room.

He was striding ahead of her down the hall, headed for the stairs. She raced after him. "Listen, Luke, since you're obviously on the mend, wouldn't this be a perfect time to come out in public—"

"And support your anti-casino groundswell, right?" he asked cynically.

"Well, now that you mention it..."

He swore under his breath. "Gilly, if I ever accuse you of having anything but a one-track mind, remind me of this moment."

"Luke, it would be so good for you," she pleaded, catching his arm to slow him down. "You need to come out of hiding sometime, don't you think?"

Carefully, with a slight wince, he detached her hand from his arm. "Not yet."

"You said you were better," she tried, scooting in ahead of him as they reached the ballroom. She had plans to launch more arguments, but then she took a look around at the remains of his nocturnal garden. "Wow, this is pretty sad." She picked up the limp frond of a once luscious palm tree. It was only one among the wounded in the collection of plants. "What happened? Not much of a green thumb, huh?"

"Obviously." He shrugged, his hands in his pockets. "It appears they weren't getting enough natural light. Even nocturnal plants need more sunlight than I was giving them."

"Huh. Well, that's interesting, isn't it?" Gilly's

eyes narrowed as she gazed around at the assortment of dejected flora. "And I hesitate to say I told you so, but you know, Luke, the lesson here for your own life isn't hard to read."

He gave her a weary look.

"I'm serious," she contended. "Just like the plants, you need light and sunshine. You can't survive shut away, either."

"Gilly..." His tone was weary, too. "Like I said, if I ever accuse you of having anything but a one-track mind—"

"Yeah, yeah, I've got it." But in fact she still didn't really get it. Luke seemed okay, if a little edgy and moody. So why did he continue to refuse to come out of the house?

She mused on the subject of agoraphobia for a second or two, wondering how people who had it behaved. Could it come up all of a sudden, after someone had spent years being the total opposite of a homebody?

"Luke?" He looked up from the cactus he was fooling with, a wary light in his blue eyes. "If you're not well and it's persisted this long, maybe you should see a doctor."

"You're forgetting something, Gilly," he returned evenly. "They threw a whole platoon of doctors at me at the hospital in Rome. They said there was nothing wrong with me, just like I told you."

"Yes, but there *is* something wrong with you." Her voice softened as her compassion grew.

She came closer, backing him against the cactus table. She reached out a hand to stroke his cheek.

"Maybe you need to see a different sort of doctor," she suggested kindly. "Someone who can get to the bottom of your feelings about your ordeal in Crete. I mean, it's no sin for someone to be experiencing some emotional fragility after an experience like—''

His voice slashed over hers, cutting her off. "I haven't lost my mind, Gilly. Not yet. Although you're pushing me closer every time I see you."

Poor thing. Of course he didn't want to admit it. She wanted very badly to hug him, but she confined herself to patting his shoulder and his cheek.

Luke looked decidedly nervous as she touched him; he seemed to have developed a slight tic in his jaw. He stood there, rigid, for several long moments, then suddenly reached out and grabbed her wrist, holding her hand away from him.

Her eyes met his, and tension crackled between them like a live wire. His hand was very warm, and she could feel his pulse jump erratically. Or was that hers?

Whoa. This was more than she could handle. Delicately she tugged her hand free and turned away, pretending they had not just shared that bizarre moment.

Touch me not, she thought. But why?

Whatever the reason he was so unwilling to be touched, she felt sure this was just further evidence of her theory. Luke was teetering on the brink of something very strange. She didn't say it out loud, but she knew her warm, sympathetic gaze told him how she felt.

"There is nothing wrong with my mind," he repeated softly, firmly.

Gilly needed to lighten this moment, if only for her own sanity. "Okay, so you're under a Minoan curse, is that it?" she asked with a laugh. But Luke didn't laugh. "I was just kidding," she continued. "You don't believe that, do you?'' Still he said nothing. "I was making it up, Luke. Like King Tut's tomb. There's no curse on King Minos's labyrinth, is there?''

"Not that I'm aware of.'' He moved away, adding to the distance between them. He picked up one of his cameras and regarded it moodily.

Gilly continued in the same jovial vein. "Well, listen, if you want to find out, we can either take a trip back to the museum—they have a nice Minoan collection—or we can call up Susie Woods, my student with the fascination for things ancient. Susie's probably ready for her master's degree in Minoan culture by now.''

"You know, I hadn't thought of that,'' Luke mused, "but it's not a bad idea.''

"Calling Susie?'' she asked doubtfully.

"No, the museum.'' He began to pace, still carrying the camera, picking up speed and energy. "Maybe I've been going about this all wrong. Instead of studying nocturnal plants, reading up on bats, trying to figure out the darkness, maybe what I should've been doing was learning about the Minotaur and the labyrinth. I mean, you're right—what if this *is* related to the damn bull?''

Well, she'd wanted to see a reaction, hadn't she? Just not this particular reaction, which made him seem even closer to the edge.

"I don't really understand any of what you just said,'' she told him slowly. "I mean, if you want to go to the museum, that's great, because at least you'd be outside for a few minutes, which could only be good, if you ask me. Blow the stink off, as my mother used to say.''

"Gilly,'' he warned, "don't dither.''

"I'm not dithering! Okay, okay, back to the point. Yes, we'll go to the museum if you want to. Just pick a time."

Carefully, trying to get there before he noticed, she edged nearer. He noticed, and slid away the very same amount. This was like a chess game with living pieces.

She continued, "Okay, so the museum would be lovely. But what's this about studying the darkness and looking for bulls? What does that mean?"

He shrugged, fussing with the settings on his camera. "I told you before, I've been looking into the effect of darkness on things—plants, bats—"

"People," she finished for him. She narrowed her gaze. *The effect of darkness on people...* Now why did that sound familiar? *He's clearly more comfortable with darkness than with light.* She snapped her fingers. "Nightshade!"

Luke jumped. "What?"

"Nightshade," she repeated. "Don't you read the papers?"

"Sometimes," he said hastily. "Why?"

"This Nightshade guy has been all over the papers for the past few days because he keeps popping up in the nick of time in West Riverside and saving people...well, saving *me*, if you want to know the truth." She knew she was blushing, and she really hated doing that in front of Luke, but she couldn't hold it back.

"Saving you? That wasn't in the papers," he noted, gazing at a point somewhere over her head.

What was with him, anyway? "Well, no, because I didn't tell them. The first time Devon Drake, the reporter, got front-and-center coverage, and the second time, they mostly focused on Mrs. Mooshman." She advanced eagerly on Luke. "But I'd really like to know who this guy is. I kind of... He kind of..."

She broke off awkwardly, absolutely refusing to even hint to Luke that she was developing a major crush on a mystery man in a black hat.

"We kind of connected," she finished lamely.

His gaze was so intent she blushed all over again. "I don't mean to pry, but I'm beginning to get the idea you have a certain fascination for this Nightshade character. A fascination of, shall we say, a romantic nature?"

Gilly gulped. "No, of course not. I've never really met him, you know, in the flesh..."

"Well, I hope not. Not in the flesh. Not yet," he commented with a rather sarcastic edge.

"Luke!" she protested. "It's nothing like that. It's just, well, you were studying nocturnal things, and he's kind of nocturnal, so I thought maybe you could help me figure him out a little better."

Luke's face was unreadable. "And why would I do that?"

"Because I asked you," she returned, stating what should've been perfectly obvious. Why was he being so obtuse? "If I understand him, maybe I could find him, and then I would know how he does this...intensity thing."

"Intensity thing?"

"Yeah." Gilly sighed, remembering.

She stared into space, no longer seeing the high ceiling of the ballroom, the wavy flowers and leaves, not even Luke. In her mind, she was back on that street corner, deep in the shadows, and Nightshade was looming over her, strong and safe and achingly real.

"He has this way of just wrapping you in his pres-

ence," she whispered, conjuring up the memory of
him sweeping her into those powerful arms, carrying
her away. "I can't really explain it—I've never met
anyone who made me feel that way before. I don't
know how he did it. I mean, he barely touched me,
and he only kissed me twice, and the second one was
just a quick peck. But man alive, I felt like I'd been
knocked off my feet by a typhoon, y'know?"

"No, I wouldn't know." Luke's voice was positively testy. "You didn't say he kissed you."

Oops. She hadn't planned to divulge that. Her
cheeks flamed. She wasn't ashamed she'd kissed him,
but it was a private thing, which she had never intended to share with anyone, and especially not with
Luke.

"I can't believe you're all gooey-eyed over some
bizarre vigilante in a Zorro costume," he fumed, and
once again, she was struck by his reaction.

"It's not Zorro at all. More like the Shadow. And
gooey-eyed? I never said I was—"

"It's written all over you," Luke retorted. He
plunked his camera on a table with such force he
must've broken it, and then savagely thrust his hands
into his pants pockets. He pulled his hands back out
with a groan of pain. "Damn," he muttered, glaring
down at his palms. "I wasn't paying attention."

"What did you do—break a nail?"

"Something like that," he growled. "But you
haven't answered me, Gilly. Why are you so intrigued
by this freak in the sunglasses?"

She ignored his question, choosing, instead, to pose
one of her own. "What do you think he's hiding,
Luke? Why would someone risk his life to save someone else and then disappear?" She shook her head

impatiently. "It's like he has a secret or something. What do you think it is?"

"Since he only comes out at night, maybe it's something glamorous like he's a vampire," he snorted. "They're in fashion these days, aren't they?"

"Well, I don't think vampires ever go out of fashion," she said after a moment of consideration. "But that wasn't what I had in mind."

"Gilly, come on! Get with the program." This time he was the one who closed the distance between them. Very gingerly he bracketed her shoulders with his hands and looked deeply into her eyes. "He's just some adrenaline junkie who gets his kicks out of lurking in the shadows and then charging out to your rescue—only you, have you noticed? Plenty of other people are mugged every day, and your hero doesn't raise a finger. Sounds more like a stalker than a hero to me," he muttered. "A nutcase."

"Lurking in the shadow and charging out to my rescue..." She threw her arms around Luke. "That's it! I know how to find him. He so much as told me all I had to do was call and he'd be there."

Luke stiffened and that tic appeared in his jaw again. "A real Four Top."

"I was thinking Henry Fonda in that old grapes movie." Gilly was too happy to care if he was being asinine. She danced away from his embrace, vaguely noticing that the tic disappeared as soon as she was gone. "But don't you see, Luke? This is so easy. All I have to do is be in danger, and presto! Nightshade will be there."

There was a long pause. "You can't be serious."

"It's perfect!"

"It's idiotic!" he countered. "You're going to put

yourself in danger on purpose just to flush out a potential date?"

"Well, when you put it that way..." She glared at him. "This is important, Luke. I need to find this guy! I've never felt—"

"Yeah, yeah. You've never felt this way before. I heard you the first time."

She propped herself on a sturdy table full of cacti, swinging her legs happily. What a great plan! Even Luke's grim mood couldn't change the fact that she had a plan and she would be seeing Nightshade again very soon. "If you'd ever met him, you would understand," she maintained fervently.

But Luke wasn't playing. "Somehow I doubt he's my type."

"It doesn't matter. He *is* my type. And I'm going to find him." Fired up with enthusiasm, Gilly headed for the door.

"What about Career Day? And the Snow Ball and all that stuff?" Luke demanded.

She turned. "What about them?"

"I thought you were here in the first place to strong-arm me into going." He sounded almost hurt she'd let him slide just this once. "I thought Benny's was going down the tubes without my help. Now you're leaving, and all I've said is no." He paused and then swooped in for the kill. "Gilly Quinn, retreating in defeat?"

"Hah!" She crossed her arms. "Who said I was defeated?"

"Listen, Gilly, I'll make you a deal," he offered softly. Once again he advanced to meet her. Once again the sparks in those blue eyes caught and held her. "If you give up this crazy idea about luring Nightshade into the open, I'll come to Career Day. I'll even throw in the Snow Ball.''

Her heart leaped in her chest. Luke, giving in? Victory, so close at hand?

"All you have to do," he went on in the same snake-charmer voice, "is be smart and play nice." He smiled, that beautiful break of white teeth between narrow, sensual lips. "No danger zones for you. Career Day and Snow Ball for me. Is it a deal?"

Gilly leaned in very close, so that her mouth was just below his ear. "No," she whispered with a puff of warm air. "Not in a million years."

And then she spun on her heel and left his shadowy ballroom.

"Gilly," he called after her, not bothering to be persuasive. Now he sounded plain old ticked off. "Give up this insane idea."

"Nope."

"So you admit defeat?" His voice rose. "I'll tell the Fitzhughs they don't have to worry anymore, because you won't be hassling either them or me ever again. Is that right?"

She wheeled back around to face him, but kept on walking. "Don't be ridiculous. You'll come around, Luke. I know. you. You'll be doing Career Day and the Snow Ball—oh, and the scholarship and maybe even a press conference—and I won't have to give up a thing."

"Don't count on it."

She gave him a beatific smile. "Just wait and see, Luke."

But his face was drawn in sharp angry lines. "If you go through with this, what I may be seeing is you in a bloody heap in a dark alley. God, Gilly, don't go through with this.''

"I won't even break a fingernail," she assured him. "Nightshade will save me."

"Nightshade will save you," Luke echoed with heartbreaking cynicism. "Why doesn't that make me feel better?"

Chapter Eight

It was still dark, but Luke had long since roused the household.

"I don't have a choice," he said grimly. "She hasn't left me any options."

"I'd like to take her over my knee," Abigail Fitzhugh sputtered from her place at the stove. "That girl always did need a firm hand. But she would grin and toss those red curls, and people would always give her what she wanted." As her husband hung back, she skewered him, too, gesturing with a spatula and a frying pan full of scrambled eggs. "And you're partly to blame, Harry Fitzhugh! Your sister spoiled her rotten, and you never said a word."

"Now, Abby, there's nothing wrong with Gilly. She's just free-spirited, that's all. Always has been," he responded in his usual gruff tone.

"Free-spirited, hah! High-handed is more like it. And now look at the trouble she's gotten poor Mr. Lucas into." Abigail filled plates with eggs and bacon and dumped them unceremoniously on the table in front of Luke and Fitz.

Fitz dug in right away, limiting his conversation, but Luke gave his plate a disdainful stare.

"Eat, Lucas," Abby ordered. "You need your strength, especially if you're going to run around after Gilly."

"I've been doing much better," he told them both.

Abigail let out another "Hah!" followed by, "And after the first time, when you were knocked off your feet by your little masquerade, anything but a coma would've been an improvement, wouldn't it?"

"The last time I appeared, I actually had very few lasting side effects," he argued. "I've been able to control almost everything, even the headaches."

"Would that be the last time you appeared as, er, Nightshade, sir?" Fitz asked with a certain dry humor.

"That wasn't my idea. The newspapers gave me the stupid nickname!" Luke pushed back from the table, losing whatever appetite he'd had. The smell of eggs and bacon was much too strong to be appealing, anyway, even when he exerted his strictest curb over his wayward senses. "What a joke. Nightshade. It sounds like I should be wearing a cape."

"Well, it has a certain ring to it, sir." Now Harry Fitzhugh was definitely making fun. His mustache quivered with suppressed glee. "Perhaps Mrs. Fitzhugh might be able to come up with a suitable outfit, sir? Your basic black panty-hose-type thing, with a flower on the front of the, er, trunks, representing deadly nightshade, perhaps?"

Luke did not appreciate being the butt of his chauffeur's jokes. "I suppose it's my own fault for wearing the coat and hat and all that. But that was to protect my eyes, my ears, my skin, not to disguise me. I had no idea this thing would boomerang and I'd become some kind of romantic icon."

Luke was at a loss. Nothing was turning out the way

he'd planned. Of course, he really hadn't planned much—just let himself get sucked in by circumstance.

"I didn't even plan to be mysterious. But the first time, it knocked me out—the lights, the noise, everything. If I'd told her who I was and the reason for the getup, she would've known about my..."

What did he call this ghastly amplification of his senses? "My powers," he said reluctantly. "And once Gilly knew about my powers, she wouldn't mean to, but she'd spill it to the whole world. There I'd be, on the front page of every tabloid in the country—Freak Accident Leaves Freak Photographer."

"I don't know, sir," Fitz began kindly, but Luke shook his head. He was even more resolute on that point now than he'd been at the start.

"Gilly is not going to know what kind of mutant I've become." He ran a hasty hand through his hair. "So I guess that means I maintain the so-called secret identity unless I can find a way to get rid of these powers once and for all. God, I'm living a super hero's life."

The burly chauffeur shrugged. "Well, you *have* started rescuing maidens in distress, sir."

"Maidens in distress!" Abigail was quivering, too, but with disapproval. "Gillian Quinn has never in her life been a maiden in distress. Iron maiden is more like it."

"Mrs. Fitzhugh, she's your niece," Luke reprimanded her. The only constants in his life were the two servants who ran his household, his relationship with his camera...and his friendship with Gilly. "I've always known I could count on Gilly when the chips were down. And she's always been able to count on me, too. That's the only reason I'm going to risk being out of control and try to nip her idiotic plan in the bud.''

"Is that the only reason, Mr. Lucas?" Abigail pursed her lips as if she had plenty more to say.

"What are you driving at, Mrs. Fitz?"

"I'm driving at something more going on between the two of you." She wiped her hands on her apron and avoided his eyes. "It's apparent to all of us—Mr. Fitzhugh and myself, that is—that Gillian has gone sweet on this Nightshade character of yours. So now it seems you're a wee bit jealous of your own alter ego."

He banged a hand on the table and immediately wished he hadn't. The sound reverberated like a deep bell inside his head. "Don't be absurd," he said between gritted teeth.

"I don't know anything about absurd, but I do know when a man is ignoring his limitations," she said smartly. "I practically raised you, young man, and I know you better than anyone. So pardon me if I'm speaking out of turn."

"You are."

"Hmph." She went on, anyway. "You are not in any condition to be undertaking a romance, especially not with the likes of Gilly Quinn, who wouldn't understand taking things easy if you hit her over the head with the rule book."

"A romance?" He was on his feet in an instant. "I never said for one instant that—"

"And what do you suppose you're doing? Taking Gilly to the museum, trying to talk to her nicely to convince her that she can't rely on this Nightshade fellow to protect her?" She rolled her eyes. "And what is that if not a jealous suitor protecting his turf?"

He knew at that moment he would never, as long as he lived, understand women. It made perfect sense to him to logically explain to Gilly, for her own good and because he was her oldest friend, that she was being an idiot. It had nothing to do with romance. He'd never felt that way about Gilly. Never.

"First of all, I am not jealous of Nightshade. He's me!" Quickly, as the sound began to vibrate in his temples, Luke lowered his voice. "And second, I am not interested in Gilly that way. I am simply trying to head her off at the pass. Developing a crush on Nightshade isn't going to bring her anything but heartbreak when she finds out he doesn't exist."

"All right." But Abigail's expression remained unconvinced. "And what happens when she tells you there is no way she is abandoning her poor dear Nightshade, as you know very well she's going to tell you?"

"I go to plan B."

"And that is?"

He didn't want to say it, but he had been forced into a corner. "I appear one more time as Nightshade, and then *he* tells her what an idiot she's being."

Mrs. Fitz threw her hands up at that one. "Sure, why not? You can appear as Nightshade again and come home shell-shocked and battered like the last two times. You do what you want, Mr. Lucas, because you're going to, anyway, but don't say I didn't warn you."

Luke appealed to Fitz; he figured he had a much better chance for understanding from the other man in the room. But Fitz wasn't getting between his wife and his boss. He wiped his mouth neatly with his napkin and rose from the kitchen table. "I'll get the car ready, sir. Give me a ring in the garage when you want to leave.''

So much for masculine solidarity.

Luke went to the phone. She picked it up on the first ring, but she sounded half-asleep.

''H'lo?''

''Gilly, it's Luke.''

''No, I'm not going to cancel my plan to catch Nightshade,'' she told him. ''Should I hang up now?''

''This isn't about that,'' he lied. ''It's about the museum. I want to take you up on your offer. I think I really need to look at the Minoan collection. Do you want to go now?''

''Luke, it's...'' He heard her roll over and pick up, then drop the clock. ''It's not even seven. The clock rolled under the bed, but I can read it from here. The museum's not open at seven on a Sunday morning.''

''You probably didn't notice, but there's a whole wing of pre-Columbian art called the Blackthorn Collection, financed by my grandfather.'' He had never used family connections before, but as long as he was taking on cloak-and-dagger missions, full of subterfuge and deceit, he might as well stoop to trading on his name, too.

''And?'' Gilly asked in a voice that sounded as if it might be muffled by a pillow.

''And I can get in any time I want. One call and we get a private tour of the museum.'' He frowned. Was she taking the bait or not? ''So when can you be ready?''

She groaned. ''I don't know, Luke. I mean, I'm not even awake yet.''

He played dirty. In a low husky voice, throbbing

with just enough desperation, he said, "Gilly, I need you."

She didn't even hesitate, but then, he'd known she wouldn't. Tell Gilly you needed her and she'd be there, no questions asked. "Give me half an hour."

"I'll pick you up at seven-thirty."

"Luke?"

"Yeah?"

Now she paused. "This means you're coming outside, right? You're coming away from Blackthorn Manor for at least a few hours?"

"It looks that way, doesn't it?"

"Good for you," she responded breathlessly, and she sounded as delighted as if she was cheering for the home team. "I'm so proud of you, Luke."

"See you in half an hour."

And he hung up, feeling incredibly guilty. Why did she have to add that last bit? It made him feel like a heel for not telling her he'd already been out, twice, and it had almost killed him. Here she was, all misty and happy, encouraging him to come out and smell the snowdrops, like it was a major stepping stone, when it would mean absolutely nothing.

He knew now there was a reason he'd never lied to her all those years. Because it made him feel like hell—the way he felt now.

"LISTEN, FITZ," he said, sliding forward in the back seat of the Cadillac limo, "as soon as you drop us off at the museum, go back and get Mrs. Fitz, and the coast will be clear."

"Yes, sir. We'll need to contact her next-door neighbor, Mrs. Mooshman, first, sir, is that correct?"

"Right. And she should be able to give you some

other names." He set his jaw. "Just in case Gilly won't go along, and I have a certain suspicion she won't...."

"Mrs. Fitz does seem to lean strongly in that direction, sir, and perhaps, as she's a woman herself, there's something to be said for her opinion."

"Better safe than sorry," Luke returned. "If Gilly doesn't go for it, I'll feel much better knowing her friends and neighbors are looking out for her."

"Exactly, sir. If they're all dogging her heels, so to speak, it will be much tougher for her to throw herself in the path of danger."

"I certainly hope so." Luke pushed back into the soft leather seat, testing it with his fingers. "Although with Gilly you can never be sure of anything."

"Here we are at her apartment, sir." Fitz doffed his cap and prepared to open his door. "I'll get Gilly and be right back."

"No, wait." Luke felt for his own handle. "I'll go."

"You'll be out in direct light for several moments, sir. You don't dare risk wearing sunglasses here."

"It's overcast enough today that I should be fine. And I'm not sending my chauffeur up to get her." *Not when I'm trying to outclass the mysterious Nightshade, king of the romantics,* he added acerbically to himself.

Even on a cloudy winter day, the natural light was painful to his eyes. Holding himself very still, he forced his body to adjust, to pull back all those throbbing sensors. Relief washed over him when it actually worked.

"Everything all right, sir?" Fitz asked from inside the car.

"Just fine." He smiled and reached for the door to her building.

He actually ran up the stairs after she buzzed him in, twitching his nostrils when he hit the landing where a residue of the smelly burglar's odor still clung. But he pushed past it.

He supposed this buoyant enthusiasm was a bit much, but he couldn't help it. He was out in the world without glasses or earplugs or mufflers, and it felt like the first day of spring.

He even knocked on her door without feeling like he'd smashed his knuckles or bruised his eardrums. Maybe he was finally learning to turn down the volume and keep it there. It required massive concentration and a state of meditation that bordered on self-hypnosis, but he was doing it, wasn't he?

Gilly swung open the door, and he caught her trademark scent, that misty lavender smell. Her lips curved into a smile when she saw him. "Luke, you're positively beaming."

"Happy to be outside, I guess."

"I told you it would do you good." She pulled back from the door, gesturing for him to come in. He saw that she was wearing a cropped brown sweater with blue jeans and funny two-toned shoes. Kind of cute and typical Gilly. Raising her chin, she said smugly, "You need to listen to me more often."

He preferred not to comment on that one. "Nice perfume," he said, instead. "Lavender. I noticed it the other evening, as well."

Her eyes widened. "But I don't wear perfume. I think there might be some lavender buried in my shampoo under oatmeal and honey or something."

She made a point of sniffing the end of one red-gold curl. "No, I don't smell anything."

Luke just shrugged, resolving to be more careful with his observations. It wouldn't do, he guessed, to let her know that there was an overripe banana somewhere in her apartment, or that he had detected the odor of a tiny spot of sweet-and-sour sauce on her counter. "I have a good nose, I guess."

"I guess."

While she got her coat and tossed things into the beat-up backpack she apparently intended to take as her handbag, he looked around. It had been a long time since he'd been in Gilly's apartment, and it had changed considerably.

It was in an older building, with dark wood trim and high plaster ceilings. In Gilly's hands, though, the apartment felt quite modern. She'd re-covered her couch in red, and there were splashes of color everywhere, from sunshine yellow pillows to a bright green table shaped like a turtle that held her television. If he hadn't dampened his senses, this room would have made his head spin.

The only thing not in color was a black-and-white photo framed and displayed on the old vanity table she was using as a desk. He recognized it immediately. Not one of his better efforts, but then he was only fifteen or so when he'd taken it. Luke picked it up, his critical eye deciding that the composition was sloppy and the light was all wrong. But he still remembered that day, and how much pure, unadulterated fun they'd had.

He had discovered the Beatles movie *A Hard Day's Night* that summer, and that had given him the burning need to do black-and-white photos of people in hip poses. It took him all day, but he finally got the camera firmly attached to the ceiling. And then he had Gilly lie on the floor underneath it. He set the timer, leaped down into the picture with her, his head opposite hers like yin and yang, and snap! Two teenagers lying on the floor looking pleased with themselves.

He couldn't believe she still had it. Gilly and Luke, captured forever on film. But the photo only strengthened his resolve. He would succeed in keeping his senses under wraps, and he would convince Gilly to stay away from Nightshade. He owed her that much.

As he turned away from the picture, he realized he had missed the most dramatic part of the apartment. The far wall had been covered with swirling paint in thick primary shades. "Somebody copy a Matisse?" he asked, stretching to remember his long-ago art classes. "Or an early Kandinsky?"

"Fielder," Gilly told him. "Tony Fielder. One of my students. He's good, isn't he?"

"Very."

"Of course," she said with a small sigh, "without St. Benny's, he'll end up sitting on the bench someplace trying to be the next Michael Jordan, instead of the next Picasso. That's the breaks, I guess."

Luke regarded her fondly, more fondly than she deserved. "You just never give up, do you?"

With a laugh Gilly poked him in the ribs. "You wouldn't love me nearly as much if I ever gave up, now would you?"

He wished he knew whether that odd hollow feeling came from her casual words or the jab to his rib cage. *You wouldn't love me nearly as much…*

Gilly, my dear, he thought, *you have no idea.* But he avoided the thought as quickly as it came.

Before she had a chance to rouse any more disturbing feelings, he herded her out of the apartment and back to the waiting car.

"Brought out the limo just for me? What did I do to deserve this?"

"It needs to get a workout, too, you know," he told her, not bothering to mention that the limousine, with its darkened windows and cushioned ride, was intended for his comfort, not hers. "The thing probably hasn't been used since before my parents died. I think my dad liked to have Fitz pick him up at the airport in it."

"Shows what you know," Gilly scoffed, settling back into the thick leather. "Aunt Abby has Fitz drive her to garage sales in it every Saturday."

"No way!"

"Way."

Luke laughed out loud. "That I've got to see."

"Hang around some Saturday and you will." Gilly leaned over eagerly. "Better yet, tell Aunt Abby you want to go with her to the next flea market. I can just see her face now. She'd have a cow!"

"I don't think I'm up to a flea market. In fact, I don't think I even know what a flea market is." He fixed her with a confused expression. "Why would anyone want to market fleas?"

"You're putting me on, right?"

Before he had decided whether or not to let her off the hook, Fitz announced that they'd arrived at the museum.

"Where are we going?" Gilly inquired. "The entrance is on Plum."

"We're special. We get to go in underneath—the private entrance." He didn't mention that they were using the delivery ramp not because they were VIPs, but because he hadn't wanted to push his luck being out in the light any more than he had to be. Coming up the long front steps to the museum's front door was rather a longer and brighter journey than he wanted to attempt.

"Hmm," Gilly murmured as the limo pulled up to the elevators underneath the museum. "First a limo and now a private entrance. If I didn't know better, I'd think you were trying to dazzle me."

Was she flirting with him? Luke didn't quite know how to handle Gilly coming on to him, even in this rather subdued fashion. "And what if I were?"

She gave him a Mona Lisa smile. "I'd have to tell you that I'm not easily impressed, certainly not by fancy cars or special privileges. In fact, they make me feel kind of guilty."

He should've guessed. Touching a finger to the tip of her snippy nose, he said, "Like all the poor people in the world are riding around on dented bicycles and there you are, all by yourself, wasting a whole limo."

"Well, exactly." She frowned. "Although it makes me sound pretty stupid when you put it that way."

"Never stupid, Gilly. Just naive." He could see she was going to bristle at that notion, so he opened the door, climbed out and held out a hand. "Come on, the Minotaur's waiting."

"I'm taking off my coat," she said. "Less to carry."

Once Gilly, minus coat, joined him, he led her upstairs into the museum proper. He hadn't been to the Riverside Museum since he was a kid, when the Blackthorn-exhibit rooms had opened. He had remembered it as a much haughtier, stuffier place. Actually it was open, modern, accessible and nicely maintained, with lighting that was subdued enough he didn't have to sweat it. Maybe he ought to look into endowing another wing with Blackthorn money, if the place didn't get torn down for the casino, that was. But surely they'd just relocate, not throw in the towel.

"The Treasures of the Ancient World are this way," Gilly told him, catching his hand and dragging him off past a sculpture garden.

The whole trip had been a ruse, really, just to get her alone. But now that he was here, he felt a bit apprehensive about actually facing Minoan artifacts. No, he didn't think he was the victim of an ancient curse on the labyrinth. The whole idea was nonsense.

But he also knew that something odd, even mystical, had happened down in that maze of subterranean corridors and dark passages. He had never delved too deeply into what exactly had propelled him down there, what higher power had given him the skills he needed to survive, to escape. He hadn't wanted to know. But now here he was, stuck with those once-welcome skills in a world where they just didn't fit comfortably. And maybe it was time to figure out where they'd come from and how to send them back.

Still, he couldn't help feeling a little uneasy about coming face-to-face with bulls again. Look what had happened the last time. He had stared at a Minoan bull, and the whole place had caved in.

As they turned into the exhibit hall, and he caught a glimpse of a large fresco with a prominent bull, he sent up the fervent hope that the museum had sturdy rafters.

"Luke!" Gilly exclaimed. "This one looks just like your photograph of the cave painting, doesn't it?"

"I haven't seen my photo of the cave painting," he said slowly. He stared at the powerful figure etched on the oversize urn she was pointing to. He might not have seen the photo, but he remembered the bull very well. Luke had stared at it for only a few moments before everything went black, but the image was imprinted on his retina.

"Well, it looks pretty much the same to me." Gilly tipped her head to one side. "Of course, your bull didn't have a half-naked lady grabbing it by the horns."

"She's vaulting over it. You know, the way Olympic gymnasts do flips over pommel horses." Luke gazed at the pottery, feeling a little ripple of déjà vu. Deep inside, he felt as if there was still some eerie chord pulling him back to the damn bull. But what did it mean? Shaking his head, trying to keep his mind on the conversation with Gilly, he managed to add, "Vaulting over bulls was their favorite sport."

"Strange sport, especially topless." Gilly flashed him a mischievous glance. "You'd think that would cause certain, ahem, logistical problems. Some things never change—the Minoan fashion industry was clearly dominated by men."

Luke smiled. "And their descendants are running Las Vegas?"

"Something like that." Her expression grew more thoughtful as she gazed at Luke, and she raised a hand in the direction of the glass case, filled with pottery and artifacts and jewelry. Farther down, there was even a man-size bust of the Minotaur. "See anything that interests you?" she asked lightly.

"I don't know." He was still uneasy, off balance.

Was he missing something? Should he be looking harder for an explanation for his strange powers?

"Luke," Gilly murmured, laying a gentle hand on his arm. "Are you all right?"

He could feel her fingers as clearly as if they were burning through the leather of his jacket. There was the pulse of life there, of human warmth and flesh and bone, seeping from her skin into his. It wasn't painful exactly, but startling and electric. He covered her hand with his own, absorbing even more of the sparks, digging deep within himself to take it, to feel it, and yet not jump back, scorched.

"It reminds you of the cave, doesn't it?" she asked. "It must have been awful, all alone in the dark."

He nodded. And yet he hadn't been thinking about the cave at all. Gazing at Gilly, with her pale, creamy skin and fiery hair, her eyes and her smile so filled with the sparkle of life, how could he think about darkness? All he saw was light, glowing from her soul, warming him with its reflection.

Light was what he needed, not darkness.

To *feel* was what he wanted, not to block it out.

And suddenly he knew without a doubt that things had changed. Gilly was still the girl he knew, but someone different now, too. Very different.

Her lips parted breathlessly, and he could hear the soft uneven rhythm of her breath, the trip of her heartbeat, smell the sunny warmth of her skin.

He wanted to kiss her more than he had ever wanted anything in his life.

Time seemed suspended between the two of them as he lowered his lips to hers, tasted the sweet luscious heat of her mouth, nibbled at her, explored her, pushed her further, drank her in.

It was intoxicating.

She made a small moan and put her arms around his neck, angling closer, and he couldn't turn back. Fiercely he pulled her to him, molding her body to his as he deepened the incredible kiss.

He could feel little sparks and jets of electricity racing from his fingertips, radiating from his mouth, blazing everywhere he touched her. It felt wonderful, yet at the same time, he knew he couldn't control it, couldn't hold it back even if he wanted to.

Gilly's arms tightened around him. Blood surged within him. She was plastered against him, with no air, no space between, and his skin burned with her nearness. Rockets exploded inside his head.

Pain. It shot out in waves from his head and his hands. Real, stabbing, excruciating pain.

He stumbled backward, pushing her away, afraid he would drop to his knees and cover his ears right there. Weak as a kitten, reeling from the agony, unable to turn it down or switch it off, he mumbled something even he didn't understand and staggered away.

He had to find his car. He had to find Fitz. He had to go home.

Now.

Chapter Nine

Fitz opened the car door as Luke came limping toward it.

"I gather it didn't go well, sir?" he inquired.

Luke winced as he lowered himself into the seat. Every muscle in his body ached, every nerve was still buzzing and snarling. "You might say that," he managed between gritted teeth. He let his head drop back and tried to focus on the ceiling, unable just yet to pull the door closed. "Did you—"

But the pain surged anew. He breathed in and out a few times. *Oh, God*. He hadn't even asked her about Nightshade or her insane plan, let alone talked her out of it.

Instead, he'd let this newfound rampant desire get the best of him. And now he was paying the price. What a disaster.

"Did you talk to the neighbor?" he asked finally. "Gilly's neighbor. Did you talk to her?"

"Yes, sir." Fitz stared down at him balefully. "Mrs. Mooshman was more than happy to take on the position of watchdog. But right now, sir, don't you think we should be worrying about you?"

"I'll be okay. I've been here before." But not this

badly. Not this intensely. He smashed a fist into his throbbing leg. *What a freak—can't even kiss a woman. Too many sensations. Pure pleasure turned to pure pain.*

"Home, sir?" Fitz asked softly, reaching down to carefully edge Luke's legs into the limo.

"Home. Please."

Fitz clicked the door shut as gently as he could, and Luke closed his eyes, trying not to feel the agony of too many nerves, too many sensations colliding in his brain. "Fitz," he mumbled. "Fitz, take me home and then come back for her."

"Yes, sir."

And the big black Cadillac pulled smoothly into the traffic.

GILLY STOOD in the Minoan exhibit, her eyes wide open, her mouth wide open, gasping for breath, unable to believe what had just transpired.

Luke Blackthorn, her dearest and oldest friend, had kissed her. And this time it was no accident. This time it was hot and sweet and so passionate it made her toes curl.

"Oh, my God," she whispered, lifting a hand to her burning cheek. *Luke kissed me.* Big time.

Her mind was racing and yet she couldn't think.

Her lungs were pushing air in triple time and yet she couldn't breathe.

"I must be losing my mind," she said out loud. She blinked, gazing around, taking in where she was for the first time in a while. "I am in an empty museum all by myself. All by myself?"

She took a few steps in the direction Luke had disappeared, but there was no sign of him or anyone else.

"He ditched me!" she concluded, shocked all over again. "He kissed me like there was no tomorrow and then he ditched me."

Angry, she marched down the still corridors toward the elevator and stabbed at the button. "I'll kill him when I see him. Okay, so it kind of took us both by surprise. That's no excuse to run out without talking it over."

She began to feel more sure of herself as the elevator doors closed in front of her. "I am composed. I am cool. I am furious!" she seethed. "We could've talked it over. Okay, sure, it's uncharted territory. But we could've hashed it out and made sense of it."

The mental image of his mouth, so hard and hot, working over hers, came crashing into her brain from out of nowhere.

"Oh, God," she groaned, bracing herself against the smooth metal wall. She swallowed. She stood tall. "Okay, so maybe we couldn't have made sense of it. But we could've tried. Running away never solves anything."

The elevator doors slid open at the basement, and Gilly strode out, ready to climb back into the limo she expected to be waiting for her, to face Luke, to act like a mature adult.

But there was no limo there. All she saw was a pair of taillights rapidly vanishing out of the ramp.

"He ditched me!" she said again, curling her hands into fists and cursing his name. "That total and complete jerk left me here with no way home!"

It took her a moment, but she managed to pull her temper back from the brink. There was nothing to kick and no one to smack, anyway, so she had no choice but to get a grip. In a cold rage, she marched out of the underground ramp, her footsteps slamming against the concrete, echoing in the empty garage.

"Horrible place," she muttered.

And Luke, her dearest friend, had just abandoned her here. She had never felt so desolate in her whole life.

When she reached the top of the ramp, walking right out onto Plum Street, the first blast of frigid winter air hit her. Suddenly she realized.

Not only had he abandoned her, he'd taken her coat!

"I'm going to kill him," she said under her breath, rubbing her arms through her soft sweater. "I'm going to put my hands around his neck and strangle him. And I'm going to enjoy it, too."

Shivering, she started down Plum Street. Nine or ten blocks to Center, three over to Beech, and then only half a block to her building. But it was freezing out here, and a medium-weight chenille sweater wasn't going to do the job.

She had no purse and no money, so she couldn't catch a cab, either, even if there were cabs to catch on this stretch of Plum Street on a Sunday morning, which there weren't.

"I'm going to kill him," she repeated by way of motivation. "If he was going to dump me, couldn't he have done it closer to my apartment? Did he have to do it here in the middle of a pretty nasty stretch of street?"

It was what they called a mixed industrial area, with a few small factories full of broken windows, a warehouse or two, some very ugly bars and a shabby apartment building. The museum, in fact, had been carved out of an old warehouse, and had been the jewel of the block ever since it opened.

This was not where she wanted to be stranded without transportation. Gilly shivered again, trying to decide whether it was worse to keep going down Plum or to try one of the side streets.

And then she got that feeling again. That watched, followed, shadowed feeling.

Not stopping to look, she picked up speed. "It's just your imagination," she told herself sharply. "You're starting to see a bogeyman behind every door."

Four blocks. Five blocks. Still the terrible weight of being pursued pressed down on her.

There was an audible crack behind her, as if someone had snapped a piece of wood in two. Stepped on something? Dropped something?

She didn't wait to find out. She started to run full out, but she couldn't make it more than two blocks. The air was too cold, and she couldn't catch her breath.

Panting, gulping, she slowed. What was she going to do?

And then it hit her. *Gilly, sometimes you are so stupid,* she berated herself. *You were supposed to be trying to put yourself in danger! Well, here you are.*

She turned around, faced right into the street and yelled at the top of her lungs, "Nightshade! Help me! I need you!"

But there was no answer. There was no tall figure in a black coat looming on her horizon, no broad shoulders, no dashing fedora.

She waited. It was only a minute or two, but the street seemed to grow colder, darker, more forbidding.

And Nightshade did not appear. Her shoulders slumped. First Luke, now Nightshade. Wasn't there anyone she could count on?

As she stood there, a long, silent limousine pulled up next to her. Uncle Fitz got out of the driver's seat and ran around to open the door for her.

"Gillian!" he chastised. "What are you doing out in the cold? Didn't you know I would come back for you?"

"I don't know anything anymore," she replied moodily. But she crawled into the back seat and wrapped herself in her coat just the same.

IF HE HAD TO LISTEN to Abigail Fitzhugh say, "I told you so," one more time, he was going to blow a fuse.

Stuck in his bed, too weak to do more than lie there and stare at the ceiling, he was at his housekeeper's mercy. "I couldn't have known how it would turn out," he muttered. Who knew that a kiss would pack more of a punch than hand-to-hand combat with thugs in an alley?

Casting an aggrieved glance at Mrs. Fitzhugh, Luke slapped on earphones and drowned her out with Chopin turned very low. But even so, he still had to see her glowering face, and he knew she was thinking it even if she wasn't saying it.

Meanwhile, his brain was a jumble of Minotaurs and emotional minefields. He had solved neither the problem of his strange supersharp senses nor the problem of his growing feelings for Gilly.

But there was nothing to be done about either. Without ESP, which unfortunately had not come with the package of senses he acquired in the labyrinth, he had no idea how to fix his nervous system run wild. Exerting steely self-control seemed to work somewhat, but not completely.

As debilitated as he was at this moment, it was obvious his attempt at meditation and mind over matter was not what you'd call a success.

And as for the other problem, well...no matter what he felt for Gilly, he couldn't act on it. If he so much as kissed her or held her, he would explode from overstimulation. Yesterday's debacle made that clear.

"I need a nursemaid, not a lover," he whispered. It was a sobering thought.

"What you need is a nice cup of tea," Mrs. Fitz said soothingly, placing a tray of tea and cookies on the bed.

What he had, no amount of tea was going to fix. He sat up, yanking off his earphones and shoving the tray aside, sloshing hot liquid into the saucer. "Bring me a phone, will you, Mrs. Fitz? I need to check on Gilly."

"Not that again," she cried, making his ears ache. "Mr. Fitz told you she was fine. That neighbor of hers, Mrs. Musselman or whatever, called this morning to report that she and some man, Mr. Zapata or something, had given Gilly a ride to school and she'd arrived safely. And Mrs. Dayton, the assistant principal at the academy, checked in around noon, and she also reported that Gilly was accounted for. We have our system of checkpoints all set up, Mr. Lucas, and it's working fine. There's no reason for you to concern yourself personally."

"Noon was five hours ago. I just want to be sure she's okay." He lowered his gaze, mumbling, "And I need to apologize."

"Apologize? You?" Mrs. Fitzhugh's eyebrows shot up so far she looked like she was going to have to retrieve them from the top of her neat little bun. "Well, I never."

"May I have the phone please?"

She went and got it, but she handed it over with a warning. "Don't talk too long. You need to conserve your strength."

"And what exactly am I conserving it for?" he returned as she left the room.

Damn invalid. He could store up all the good behavior points from here to the North Pole and it wouldn't do him any good. He still wouldn't be able to make love to a woman until he was in his dotage.

Oh, I could do it all right, he thought. *If I wanted the top of my head to blow off.*

He turned on the cellular phone and dialed her home number, figuring she should've been home from school hours ago. But it rang and rang, with no answer.

He buzzed his silent alarm to get Mrs. Fitz back up there. "What's her neighbor's number?" he demanded.

"The Marchmane woman?" She pulled a small spiral notebook out of her apron pocket. "Here it is. She's the first one on the list under Operation Gillian Watch."

Luke raised an eyebrow. "Operation Gillian Watch?"

"I had to call it something, didn't I?" His housekeeper scooted the tea tray back under his nose. "That Mrs. Minniver is the first one."

"It's Mooshman," he told her, "as you well know." He dialed while she eavesdropped shamelessly. He did his best to make it a quick call, but Mrs. Mooshman was quite chatty. Finally he hung up and relaxed against the pillows. "Very chatty. And very loud."

"And what did she have to say?"

"That Gilly rarely gets home from work before six." He handed Mrs. Fitz the tray and motioned for her to leave. "She gave me the number at school, so I'm going to call her there."

Luke waited until Abigail had cleared the doorway and he was sure she wasn't hovering outside in the hall. At least pinpoint hearing was good for something.

Gilly picked up the phone on the second ring. "Ms. Quinn," she said wearily.

"Gilly, it's Luke."

There was a pause. "I should hang up on you after what you did to me yesterday."

"I'm sorry. I was...ill."

"That's what Uncle Fitz told me. Convenient. Besides, it's hardly comforting to hear that kissing me made you sick."

"It wasn't kissing you," he lied. "It's...whatever it is I've been dealing with the past few weeks. Like a virus or something."

"Great, and you gave it to me."

He had never heard Gilly sound so cool, so testy. Sure, she'd been angry with him before, but it usually blew over quickly. And her anger had never had this cold, hard, final quality to it. Luckily she let in a glimmer of hope with her next words.

"Well, you do sound terrible," she allowed.

Was that sympathy he detected? He grinned. "I said I was sorry, Gilly, I tried to tell you I shouldn't leave the house, but you pushed me."

"Oh, so now this is my fault. Luke, you're unbelievable!"

Spitting-mad Gilly he could deal with. "You do have to take part of the blame," he said, enjoying the steam he could hear rising from the other end of the phone.

"Me? Was I the one who left you in the lurch without a word of explanation in an empty museum at the crack of dawn with no ride and no coat?"

That qualified as steam, all right. He felt much better to be on familiar turf again. If they were fighting, they were still friends, and back on secure footing. For a moment he could pretend that the kiss and its aftermath had never happened.

"I sent the car back, so you had a ride," he argued. "And who expected you to take off on foot without a coat? You could've waited."

"Oh, forget it," she snapped. "You're impossible. Listen, I have work to do. What are you doing calling me at school, anyway? I'm busy."

"Sounds pretty quiet."

"Of course it's quiet. I'm the only one here."

No, you're not. She couldn't hear it, but he could. Even over the telephone wires, the sound of rushed breath and stealthy footsteps came across clear as a bell.

"Are you sure there's no one else there?"

"Of course I'm sure. There's a basketball game over at Luther North tonight. It's the regional final or something important, and everybody is there. I'm the only one here."

So why did he sense danger so near to her? He couldn't have said how he knew or why his strange skills worked this way, but where Gilly was concerned, his powers of discernment were uncanny, unparalleled.

Luke concentrated, picturing Gilly sitting at her desk in the middle of the Benedict Academy. He pulled together every ounce of his sensory ability and focused on Gilly. He smelled erasers, floor wax, dusty rooms. He sensed her heartbeat, her familiar lavender scent. And the threat of someone just outside her office.

"Gilly, lock your door and stay in your office," he said hurriedly.

"What are you talking about?"

"I could hear someone in the hallway while we were talking. Loud footsteps," he lied. "Didn't you hear them?"

"It's probably just the janitor," she said. But he could hear the edge of uncertainty in her voice. "Listen, Luke, I have to go."

"Lock the door and stay where you are."

"Luke, I'm at St. Benny's," she protested. "In other words, a safe haven. No one would try anything here."

Was she really that naive or just pretending?

"I'll just go see what the noise is and call you right back, okay?"

"No, don't hang up!"

"Okay. I'll leave the phone right here and you can listen."

He didn't tell her he didn't need the damn telephone to listen. She was already gone. *Damn.* Luke threw the phone across the room, creating a loud crash that echoed in his brain. "Damn her, anyway. She's probably doing it on purpose because she thinks Nightshade will show up. It didn't work the last time, either, Gilly. I could hear you perfectly, but I was in no condition to get there."

Unfortunately he was still just as incapacitated.

Frustration burned in him. But he reached for his buzzer.

"Fitz, get up here!" he yelled, paying no attention to the damage he was doing his ears. When Fitz entered the room seconds later, Luke said, "Nightshade has to make an appearance and I can't get there. So you'll have to go. Put on the coat and the hat and the sunglasses, and even if she sees you, she won't know the difference."

"What?"

"Just do it," he ordered. "The coat and the hat are on the other side of my closet. Go get them now. Come on, man, we don't have time to stand around. Gilly's at the school and some maniac is breathing down her neck."

"You're sure about this, sir?"

He could feel the adrenaline rush already starting to sap him, and he slumped into his pillows. But he could still smell Gilly's lavender shampoo, still hear the sound of her pursuer's rushed breathing. "Just do it. And give me back the phone, will you?"

GILLY'S INTERNAL ALARMS were ringing like crazy. Luke was right; even if she hadn't heard the footsteps, she knew there was someone out in the hall.

Her heart beat a shade faster as she turned the knob and slowly eased the door open. She edged out carefully. But the hall was quiet and dark, just an endless series of closed lockers and doors. She heard an ominous creak and she whirled, but it was just the old pipes in the place, squeaking as the furnace kicked in.

She breathed out a sigh of relief, setting a hand over her heart to stop its racing. And that was when the hand grabbed her.

She fought it, but her assailant shoved a rag in her mouth and she began to gag. His other arm circled her neck, dragging her backward, choking her.

She sagged as much as possible to make herself a dead weight and dug in her heels.

"Cut the crap, lady," the vicious voice snarled in her ear. "Ain't nothin' gonna happen to you. This time."

She tried to cry out, to ask who he was or what he wanted, but she couldn't get any words past the gag.

He chuckled and leaned closer, and she could feel the hot puffs of his breath ruffle her hair. "But you be sure and call the police to report this, y'hear? And you be sure and tell that cute little blondie reporter friend of yours, because we like seeing stories about us in the paper."

He tightened his grip on her neck as he yanked open the door of the janitor's closet. Gilly could smell the mop bucket and the acrid scent of cleaning supplies.

"This is just a friendly warning. Maybe you shouldn't oughtta be such a do-gooder, huh? Maybe a lower profile for you would be a damn fine idea."

And then he shoved her, hard, into the closet and slammed the door shut.

The first thing she did was rip the rag out of her mouth and throw it on the floor, kicking it into the far reaches of the closet. "Hey!" she cried, pounding on the door. "Let me out of here!"

But there was no one to hear her. No one but Nightshade.

"You didn't come the last time," she whispered. "I called and you didn't come. But what have I got to lose?"

She took a deep breath, gathered all her vocal power

and screamed, "Nightshade!" at the top of her lungs. As if by magic, the door swung open. She raced out, ready to greet her rescuer, but all she caught was a glimpse of the black flap of his coat as he cleared the front door.

"Damn!" she swore. "He disappeared again."

She raised both hands to her face, pushing her hair back, wishing she could block out what had just happened.

"And it happened at St. Benny's." That was the worst. The safe haven for the whole neighborhood had been violated. Then she remembered she'd left Luke hanging on the phone, and she raced back into her office to fill him in.

"Some creep threw me in the janitor's closet, just so I'd call the police or something," she told Luke, her voice a mix of fear and relief. "I really didn't understand any of it. But the important thing is that Nightshade showed up to save me, just like I told you he would."

"So you think your plan worked?" Luke asked icily.

"Not exactly. I mean, Nightshade didn't stick around or leave any calling cards or anything." Her confidence and good humor were returning now that she was free of her attacker. "So I guess he remains a mystery."

"Surely you're not going to hang around dark alleys or whatever insane plan you have in mind just to see him again." Luke's voice was ragged and low, but she could hear the thread of fury in it. "This little escapade ought to have demonstrated that you can't put yourself in that sort of situation."

"Nothing happened," Gilly assured him. "Except

that I got locked in a closet for about a second and a half.''

"Gilly, give it up."

"No," she told him firmly. "I have to see him again."

If Luke had said anything about that kiss they'd shared, if she hadn't been so wounded by the way he'd just taken off, she might have listened. But not this way. Not this time.

She could hear the depth of his sigh over the receiver. "Listen, I have to go," he said softly. "Fitz just got back from an errand I sent him on and I want to know how it turned out." There was a pause. "Do you have a ride home? I can send Fitz for you."

"I don't need you sending Uncle Fitz for me," she said smartly. "As it happens, Mr. Zamechnik and Mrs. Mooshman are on NOD Squad patrol tonight, and they offered to come by and pick me up around six. I'll be perfectly safe."

"You'd better be."

"Good night, Luke."

As she dropped the receiver into the cradle, she pondered what that was all about. All these years she'd thought she understood Luke Blackthorn perfectly. But these days he kept throwing her curve after curve.

"Either I never understood him in the first place, or he changed completely in that damn cave." She propped her chin on one hand and stared into space. "I wonder what really happened down there. I wonder if he'll ever tell me."

Just then the phone rang under her hand. "Hello?"

"Ms. Quinn, this is Devon Drake. I just got an

anonymous tip that you were attacked and held captive tonight at your school. What can you tell me?''

"News travels fast," Gilly said under her breath. "Well, listen, Ms. Drake, it's like this..."

Chapter Ten

"All I really did was open the door, sir," Fitz reported dutifully. He had taken off the sunglasses and the scarf, but he was still wearing the coat and the fedora. Since Luke wore protective padding under the coat, making him look broader and bulkier, Fitz at his natural unpadded size was a good match for Nightshade. "I attempted to follow the perpetrator, but he eluded me, sir."

"Damn. I wish I knew what this was all about. Do you think it's really just that West Riverside is going to hell in a handbasket?" Luke set his jaw. "Or does somebody have something specific against Gilly?"

"The neighborhood does seem to be getting worse, sir." Fitz mopped his florid brow with a handkerchief. "I've been following it in the newspapers, and there do seem to be more muggings and robberies than usual. But this tonight…well, sir, I do wonder if Gilly hasn't stepped in it—you should pardon the expression, sir—with this anti-casino stance she's adopted."

"That's what I thought. A little creative criminal activity to make West Riverside look like the perfect place to tear down," Luke said softly. "And to scare Gilly into shutting up. Except they don't know Gilly very well if they think that'll do any good." He would've laughed if it didn't hurt so much.

"Exactly, sir."

"Which means we'd better keep up Operation Gillian Watch." Luke cast a sly glance at Abigail. "That is what we're calling it, isn't it, Mrs. Fitz?"

"Yes, it is, Mr. Lucas, as you well know," she said stiffly.

"All right, then. You go back on the watch, Fitz, and let me know if anything unusual happens. I," he noted uncomfortably, "am going to try to get some sleep."

"A very good idea, Mr. Lucas." Abigail fluffed his pillows and tucked him in while he glowered at her. He didn't need to be treated like a three-year-old. Come to think of it, he hadn't been cosseted like this even when he *was* three. "We'll see you in the morning, sir," she crooned.

In the morning. If all hell hadn't broken loose by then.

THERE WAS NO CLOCK in his room, but Luke could tell by the amount of light seeping in around his heavy curtains that it was well past morning.

"I must've slept a whole night and day away," he mumbled. He'd never been a big sleeper, and this had to be a personal record of some kind. He should've been groggy or achy, but he wasn't. In fact, he felt better than he had in days.

He sat up, blinking. The room was dim and quiet; no errant noises from outside assaulted his ears. He popped out his earplugs. He could pick up more, but nothing terribly invasive.

"Maybe sleep is the answer," he said doubtfully,

flexing one leg tentatively. No answering shriek of muscle against bone against nerve. He stood up, took a few strong strides. No pain. He really *was* better.

A few hours in the sensory-deprivation tank, and he'd be good as new.

"I thought I heard you up and about," Mrs. Fitz said, nudging open the door with her hip as she brought in a breakfast tray. "Feeling better, are we?"

"Your hearing is better than mine," he said dryly. "What time is it, anyway?"

"Almost nine."

"P.m.?"

"Yes, p.m." She frowned, setting the tray down on the foot of the bed. "Something to eat, sir?"

"No, thanks," he murmured, distracted by the feel of his hand as he made a fist and let it go. A tingle perhaps, more than a normal person felt, but no sharp fallout from bundles of nerve endings.

Mrs. Fitz picked up the tray and moved it to right under his nose. "You're going to want to see this, sir."

"A sandwich?"

"The newspaper, sir. Gillian has made the news."

He snatched it up and scanned the front page. Under the banner headline "Search for Nightshade Continues," they had repeated that same ridiculous sketch. "Black Bart at the OK Corral," Luke said derisively. Quickly he read the accompanying article.

Gillian Quinn, an elementary schoolteacher at the Benedict Academy in West Riverside, may well be the "emotional connection" forensic psychologist Arthur Dent noted in his Nightshade profile.

Quinn notes that she has been present at each appearance of the mysterious West Riverside vigilante. "I don't know whether he is a former student of mine or perhaps just someone who agrees with me that the mayor's plan to destroy our neighborhood for a casino is a terrible idea," Quinn said. "But he knows me, that's for sure."

"What is she doing?" Luke cried. "'He knows me, that's for sure'? Is it open season on Nightshade all of a sudden? Or open season on Gilly?"

The article continued:

Police have indicated that they would be interested to know Nightshade's real identity, but that it is not a priority at this time since he has committed no crime, but instead, stopped several. "We don't encourage people to take the law into their own hands, but in an area as bad as West Riverside, every little bit helps," said Police Commissioner Ronald Segretti.

"Oh, great. Gilly gets in her zinger about the mayor, but they still find a way to bash the neighborhood." Luke shook his head. "I guess we can add Commissioner Segretti to our list of stooges on the mayor's payroll."

"Read on, Lucas," Mrs. Fitz commanded. "You haven't gotten to the worst part yet."

"It gets worse?"

"Since the police are not willing to locate Nightshade, I will have to do it myself," Gillian Quinn said Sunday.

"Oh, Gilly..." he murmured, but he couldn't avert his eyes from the paper.

"I'll camp out in every dark alley in West Riverside if I have to, but I know he'll come."

"Like waving a red flag," Luke said grimly. "Gilly, what in the hell do you think you're doing?"

"We've already talked to everybody on Operation Gillian Watch, and they're all on alert," Mrs. Fitzhugh was quick to assure him. "No need to panic."

He wasn't panicking. He was furious. Luke stormed into the closet and shoved aside the false back, pushing into the secret passageway.

"Luke, what are you doing?" his housekeeper demanded, crowding in after him. "You can't mean to—"

"If she wants Nightshade, Nightshade is what she gets." He stopped at the small storage room off to one side, delving into a trunk for the old padded hockey uniform his grandfather had worn when he was young. He started to drop his pajama bottoms. "Staying around for a show?"

"No, of course not." Mrs. Fitzhugh skedaddled, but he could hear her hovering in the bedroom outside the closet, pacing, fretting.

He dragged on the padded pants and jersey, pulled black warm-up pants on over that and finally grabbed the long black coat and fedora off the broad oak coatrack in the corner.

The scarf and gloves hung there, too, while the final piece of the Nightshade costume, the sunglasses, lay in the coat pocket.

His arms full of Nightshade paraphernalia, he swept back into the bedroom for his earplugs.

"You can't do this!" Mrs. Fitz protested. "You'll make yourself ill again."

He thumped his chest. "I'm covered. Flying pucks didn't put a scratch on grandfather, and nothing will hurt me, either."

"Think about last time—"

"Last time I was completely unprotected. This time I've got the whole shebang." He opened his palm, revealing the earplugs. "I went out before this way, you know. I picked her up, I carried her, I kissed her, I even fought with a burglar, and I was fine afterward. Apparently all this protective covering muffles my senses enough to let me get away with things I otherwise couldn't."

"You kissed her? You carried her?" Abigail's mouth dropped open. "You never told me any of that!"

"Why would I?"

"Mr. Fitz! Mr. Fitz!" she cried, running out into the hall. "I told you there was a romance brewing here. He kissed her!"

In what was becoming a habit, Luke pushed in his earplugs, shrugged on the coat and tucked the scarf around his neck. He strode for the bedroom door, tugging on his gloves, just in time to meet Fitz, who was racing up the stairs. Luke stopped.

"Just so we all have our stories straight," he announced. "I have now kissed her four times, twice as Nightshade and twice as myself. And I'm not sorry. Well, actually I am kind of sorry about the last time, because it didn't work out well. But otherwise I'm not sorry at all. Is there a romance brewing? No. There can't be. It would be pretty tough to romance someone in this outfit." He threw out his arms to give them a good look at his padded getup. "And without it, I can't even touch her. It blows my circuits."

"Luke, please don't go. You're too...fragile," Abigail Fitzhugh pleaded.

"I will be careful. I will be fine." He squeezed past her and her husband. "Don't worry, Fitz. I'll drive myself this time."

The chauffeur cleared his throat. "Uh, sir? You might want to wear shoes."

All three of them stared at Luke's bare feet, poking out from under all those layers of black clothing.

"Shoes. Excellent idea."

GILLY WAS TAKING approximately her fifteenth phone call of the evening. "Yes, Suzette, yes, I'll have that report to you tomorrow. First thing. I promise."

The doorbell rang and Gilly said hastily, "Doorbell. Gotta go. Bye, Suzette."

Running a hand through her curls, she crossed to the door as the person on the other side continued to lay a heavy hand on the buzzer. Who now, for goodness sake? A peep through the hole told the story. Mrs. Mooshman again.

"Mrs. M, I thought I told you—" she started, swinging open the door.

"Look, honey, I brought you some muffins."

"How sweet." Gilly took the plate, sniffed appreciatively, but couldn't really smell the muffins under their heavy coat of plastic wrap. "Thank you. I'd invite you in, but I have to get back to work. I didn't even plan to be in tonight, but the assistant principal just assigned me a surprise report that I have to do right away, so I'm in kind of a rush.''

"Sure, sure, I understand." Mrs. Mooshman's eyes filled with a rather determined light. "But if you go out, bring back my plate, okay? I might, uh, need it right away. So come and check, all right, darling? Just if you go out. That's all I'm saying."

Mystified, Gilly gazed down at the dish Mrs. M was so attached to. It looked like just a regular dinner plate. "Well, sure, if you need it back," she said vaguely as she closed the door on Mrs. Mooshman. Shaking her head, she retreated to her kitchen and immediately peeled off the wrap and stuck the muffins on a plate of her own. Just in case.

She had no sooner sat back down to her report than the phone rang again. She stared at it balefully, but finally deigned to pick it up.

"Hi, Mrs. Fielder. What a surprise. Yes, Tony is doing fine. No, no more incidents. Yes, just fine."

She nibbled on her lip, waiting for her student's mother to get to the point. Mrs. Fielder had never called before just to chat. And this wasn't a good time to start a new habit.

"Maybe we should make an appointment sometime during school hours, Mrs. Fielder, when we can discuss this more fully. It's just that I'm a little tied up right now. Okay, sure. No, no problem. If you'd like to talk right now, I'd be happy to."

Bzzzz. The doorbell. Again?

"Look, Mrs. Fielder, that's my doorbell. Can I get back to you? Oh, you'll hold? Okay."

She felt like screaming. Why had every person she'd ever met decided to show up tonight?

This time she tore open the door with a bit more

force, catching sight of Mrs. Mooshman rapidly closing her door across the hall. Spying? What for? Turning to her latest visitor, resplendent in his bright green NOD Squad warm-up suit, Gilly offered, "Hi, Mr. Zamechnik. What are you doing here?"

"I've been taking a class over at the senior citizens center and I made you this." The old man held up a pretty, pseudo-stained-glass sun catcher that looked suspiciously like the ones on sale at the Five-and-Ten last week. "Would you like I should come in and hang it up for you?"

She narrowed her gaze. Muffins and now knick-knacks? What was *with* the neighbors?

"That's just lovely, Mr. Zamechnik. Sure, come on in. I'm not going to get anything done, anyway, I can tell."

So Mr. Z trudged to the window to fasten his trinket, while Tony Fielder's mother was still hanging on the phone, waiting for Gilly to get back.

"Mrs. Fielder, here I am," she said into the receiver. "Oh, it was my neighbor. He came over to hang up something for me. Yes, Mr. Zamechnik. I didn't know you knew Mr. Zamechnik."

If she hadn't already decided she'd fallen down a rabbit hole into Wonderland, this would've put her over the top. Tony's hardworking mother, who was in night school training to be a nurse, was pals with cantankerous old Mr. Zamechnik, who never went anywhere except to play checkers at the senior citizens center or to bother Mrs. Mooshman.

"Okay, then, Mrs. Fielder. I'll talk to you later."

"Oh, was that Tony's mother?" Mr. Z inquired, turning away from his laborious attempt to tie a string around her window latch. "Nice lady."

"How are you and Mrs. Fielder acquainted?"

"Oh, well, the, uh, NOD Squad. She just joined," he said agreeably.

"I see." But she didn't see. Tony's mother no more had time to be on the NOD Squad than fly to the moon.

As she pondered the problem, the doorbell rang again.

"Grand Central," she muttered. "Mrs. Mooshman again. What a surprise."

"Well, I couldn't help but notice that *he* was here, and I didn't want you to have to entertain the imbecile, seeing as how you're so busy. So I brought you some more muffins."

Another dinner plate full of muffins. How nice. Gilly found a smile and a thank-you as Mrs. Mooshman barged right in.

"Now what are you doing with that thing? Your string is too long," she declared, pushing poor Mr. Z aside. "Don't I have sun catchers in all my windows? Don't I know? Now where's your little suction cup?" She stared at him. "You don't have a suction cup?"

Gilly went back to her report as the battle raged on behind her. The phone rang twice, but she didn't pick it up either time.

Knock, knock. "Let's see," she said out loud, counting off on her fingers. "Unless my mom or Aunt Gert took a flight back from Florida this morning, I've already seen or heard from every single person I know."

"Gilly, it's Suzette," a voice called from the other side of the door. "I have some papers you may need for that report."

As Gilly made for the door, Mrs. Mooshman and

Mr. Zamechnik both threw themselves in front of her. "Check, see who it is," Mrs. M hissed, as Mr. Z peered into the peephole. To Gilly, the old woman chided, "You should always check first, Gilly. Check and be safe."

Gilly just stood there, her hands on her hips, giving them the once-over. "I recognize her voice. Are you going to let her in, Mr. Zamechnik?"

"Somebody could disguise a voice. It's so easy, Gilly, I saw it on TV," Mrs. Mooshman said, fluttering her hands.

Meanwhile, Mr. Z finally consented to open the door for Suzette, who burst in with a whole sheaf of papers.

"Hey, Gilly, sorry to bother you, but here are those documents we talked about."

Gilly thumbed through a few of them. "We didn't talk about any of this stuff, and it doesn't look to me like these have anything to do with my report."

"Oh. Dear." Suzette was not a terribly good liar. "Well...I..."

Gilly would've waited her out to see what lame story she came up with, but the doorbell rang again.

Her three visitors just looked at one another as if they thought someone else should go first.

"I'll get it," Gilly said sweetly, sidestepping them neatly and pulling it open. "Tony and his mom," she called out over her shoulder. "Bearing cookies. Anyone else I should be expecting? Should I just leave the door open?"

The whole gang of them exchanged sheepish looks.

"So what is this?" Gilly asked finally. "You know, it isn't my birthday, and I can't imagine any other reason for all this attention."

"Well," Suzette ventured, "we all saw the article in the paper, Gilly, and we were a little worried."

"So you decided to stage round-the-clock surveillance?" Gilly bit her lip to keep from laughing. "Well, listen, folks, I appreciate the concern. But you're busted. Everybody out, okay? I can handle things from here."

They tried to protest, but she shoved them out, thanking them profusely. "I'm not going out tonight, I promise. As soon as I shut this door, I'm going to lock it and that will be that. I'm going to take the phone off the hook, too, so no more calls and no more visitors. Bedtime for me. I'll see whoever is on duty in the morning. I assume that's you, Mrs. Mooshman?"

The older woman nodded unhappily.

"All right, then. Good night, everyone!"

She had never been so happy just to be alone in her apartment.

It was sweet, really, that they were all so concerned, but nothing was going to happen. So she had tried to flush out Nightshade. Big deal. What was the danger in that?

"Well, maybe that comment about hanging out in dark alleys was excessive," she reflected as she turned out the lights in the living room and padded into the bedroom. "Now I just have to figure out how to make it look like I'm in danger when I'm really not so I can get Nightshade to come calling. Hmm...sort of like having your cake and eating it, too."

She gave the problem a bit of thought as she brushed her teeth and changed into her nightgown, imagining what she would say and do if she could just get him alone for a few minutes.

Who are you? How do you wrap me around your finger without even opening your mouth?

Not the best opening gambit.

IT WAS A DARK moonless night, but to him it was as bright as day. He waited there on the fire escape, tinkering with the window. But the latch was broken and gave way easily, without more than a simple tug.

Balanced on the fire escape, he eased the window open, waiting, listening for any untoward sounds. All he heard was Gilly's breathing, steady and soft, coming from the bed, the buzz of her refrigerator from the kitchen, a creaky water pipe somewhere in the building.

Noiselessly he stepped inside.

It was dim and shadowy in her bedroom, but that was no obstacle. Behind his sunglasses, he focused his eyes. It was odd how much like a zoom lens they could be. It took a second to concentrate, to tune them properly, but once he did, he could see every freckle on Gilly Quinn's pretty little nose.

She lay there, her covers partially thrown back, one slim leg exposed. Her hair, that bright halo of fire, flowed over her pillow, her lashes fanned against her cheeks, and her soft luscious lips were parted in sleep.

As he watched, mesmerized, she tossed restlessly, and her nightgown—more like a big T-shirt, really—rode higher on her perfect white thigh. Lucas's mouth went dry. He wanted to trace the line of that thigh so badly his fingers pulsed inside their cashmere gloves.

It only got worse. She rolled over onto her back, sighing, murmuring dreamy words, extending a hand into the pillow over her head. The sleepy movement was innocent enough, but it arched her round high breasts, pushing the buds of her nipples up against the fabric of her shirt.

Desire surged inside him. Pleasure and pain wound together inextricably.

He could hear the raggedness of his own breathing, and he had to clamp down fiercely. He couldn't do this right now. He couldn't do this ever.

But there she was, a drowsy, sleep-tousled vision, soft, vulnerable, achingly erotic. It was beyond foolish, beyond risky, but he couldn't help imagining what it would feel like to join her on the bed, to fill his hands with her breasts, to tease those nipples into hard peaks of desire. And then he would pull her into his arms and taste her sweetness, and when she was trembling with need, he would wrap her legs around him and plunge into her so far he would never leave.

"Oh, God," he said, but his voice was no more than a raspy moan.

Gilly awoke at the sound. "What's that?" She sat up abruptly, clasping her pillow to her chest. "Who is it?"

Without saying anything, Luke moved away from the window, closer to the bed, closer to the danger zone.

"Nightshade," she whispered. Her voice had such an edge of erotic wonder he wished the name were really his.

"I saw your words…in the paper," he managed with difficulty. "I came to tell you—"

"Don't say anything." She slid to the edge of the bed, rose to her knees and looped her arms around his neck as he tried to backpedal. But she held him fast. "I knew you'd come for me."

He had to steel himself, had to pretend he was in

Antarctica and he was freezing, just to try to cool his rapidly rising ardor. *Mind over matter,* he told himself shakily, but it wasn't working. No matter what he said, no matter how rigidly he held himself, he could feel her warm pliant breasts pressing against him through all those layers of clothes, could smell her hair and her skin and her mouth, even the faint scent of her deepest secrets.

He filled his nostrils. It was tantalizing, captivating.

"No," he said roughly, trying vainly to detach her arms from around his neck.

"Oh, Nightshade," she moaned, tipping up her face to find his lips, scorching him with a wet, sinfully sweet kiss. "You are so wonderful."

"I'm not wonderful," he protested. "I'm not anything." *Focus, focus.* He closed his eyes and blocked his nose and his ears. "I came to tell you that I won't be rescuing you anymore. I can't. So please don't put any more ultimatums in the newspaper. Because I won't answer."

"Yes, you will." With a self-satisfied smile, she rose and kissed him again, reaching for his arms and pulling them around her. She slid her hands inside his scarf, cupping his face with her smooth, tender hands. "You feel the same way I do."

What he felt was on fire. The one place where she touched him—skin to skin—was his face, and his jaw tickled and twitched. But even through the cashmere, his fingers felt the hot velvet texture of her skin. *Just one touch,* he told himself, sinking fast. *Just one touch.*

He slid his hands around her ribs, barely grazing her but memorizing every inch. His sensitive hungry fingers tested, teased the curved undersides of her breasts, as he nibbled on her lips.

She gave a tiny moan, pressing closer, and he was lost, taking her breasts full in his palms, brushing her impudent nipples with his gloved thumbs.

Even deadened with so many layers of protection, his senses were alive and kicking. She seemed to have invaded his brain and his skin, and she was setting off sparks everywhere—her desire-soaked scent, her shivery whispers, her small, hot hands....

"Very clever hands," she whispered. "But I want to feel the rest of you, Nightshade. The real you." Her hands played with his collar. "Let's take this off, shall we?"

He stiffened. He couldn't do this. He knew, deep in his heart and his soul, that to toss off his clothes and take this ride would very probably kill him.

"I can't," he whispered.

One more staggering sensation, and he was going to explode.

Stifling debate with one last kiss, he pushed her back onto the bed and fled out the window.

Chapter Eleven

Alone on the bed, Gilly pressed the pillow over her face to keep herself from screaming with frustration and anger. Anger at herself, not him.

She couldn't believe how she'd just behaved. She'd been wanton, disgusting, and he'd *turned her down*.

"I am totally humiliated," she announced to the ceiling. "Why did I do that? A guy comes through the window and I start crawling all over him. Why, why, why?"

The ceiling wasn't providing answers unfortunately. "I know better," she told herself. "I know better than that. I don't sleep with just anybody. I am the most picky, healthy, cautious woman alive in the nineties. But some phantom waltzes off the fire escape, and I melt into a puddle at his feet. Men do not find puddles attractive. I know this."

She swung herself out of bed and went into the bathroom to splash cold water on her face. "What do I care if he doesn't find puddles attractive?" she asked the mirror. "Hasn't everyone been telling me I have no business lusting after some guy whose name I don't even know?

"This I promise you," she vowed to her reflection.

"I am not wasting another minute thinking about Mr. Nightshade. He can go rescue somebody else for a change!"

But as she clicked off the light and stepped back into the bedroom, she heard the window slide open.

"Back so soon?" she asked smartly, hope burning inside her despite her promise.

But it wasn't him.

Gilly swallowed her fear, not moving.

No, it wasn't Nightshade. It was a small wiry man with a dirty bandanna tied around his hair, a black leather jacket dripping with chains, ripped jeans. She recognized him. Punk number two, the one with some vague grasp on reality, the one who'd run away from the alley.

"So how's it hangin', babe?" he asked with a short, ugly laugh. "Miss me?"

She didn't speak, didn't flinch, but carefully scanned the vicinity for a possible weapon as he moved closer.

"I'm guessin' that means you ain't so glad to see me. That hurts my feelings, y'know." He was holding his knife straight up, blade out, flicking his thumb against the razor-sharp edge in time with his words. "'Cause you and me got old business to settle, don't we, babe?"

His words barely reached her; her brain was working on automatic pilot. There had to be a weapon here somewhere. *Can't reach the lamp, nail polish won't help, aspirin no good, might be able to stab him with an earring, brass book end... Perfect.* She pretended to lean against the bookshelf, her hand slowly reaching, closing over *The Thinker's* brass bottom.

"What do you want?" she asked evenly, waving her other hand in feigned agitation to distract him.

"Me and you, we could've had a little fun if you weren't so mouthy, y'know? You ain't so bad without your clothes. Still—" he edged closer "—I got a message to deliver and then I gotta go." He grinned. "Maybe another time you and me, we could have a little fun. Yeah, you'd like that. But this time, hey, I got no time for games. It's a real shame."

So far she was very proud of herself for neither trembling not screaming, for not showing this piece of crud what she thought of him. "A real shame. So what's the message?"

"It's very easy. You listen hard, okay, so I only gotta tell you once." He bent nearer so he could whisper in her ear, and she tensed, tightening her grip on the brass bookend.

Was she coordinated enough to swing it off the shelf and brain him with it before he could get the knife up? She waited, not sure. "Go on," she commanded. "Say whatever you have to say and get out."

"Here's the deal. You stop all your committees, you stay away from the city council, you don't even think about no more pep rallies and press conferences." He smiled, his lips making a smacking noise in her ear. "See, it's easy—you just stop making a pest of yourself."

"Sure," she breathed. "I got it."

"Good." And then he began to back away. Gilly remembered to breathe and her fingers relaxed on the weapon. Could it be this easy? Was he really going to leave?

He stuck a foot out the window. "Hey, while you're at it, you tell them old people in the green getups—

them NOD Squad guys—to retire, will you? I don't like old people. They bother me."

Gilly said nothing, counting the seconds until he was gone, figuring the precise number of steps it would take her to reach the phone. *Get out of here!* she wanted to shout. But she held her tongue.

He turned. "Oh, and one more thing. Tell your boyfriend Nightshade to stay off our turf, will ya? Last I heard," he said with a sneer, "sunglasses ain't no shield against bullets."

And then he was gone. Gilly raced to the window and slammed it shut, dragging her dresser over in front of it to block the way. She really *ought* to get the latch fixed.

Adrenaline was still pumping through her veins, and she was shaking so hard she couldn't even dial the number. But somehow, without even thinking about who she was calling or why, she managed to tough it out.

"Luke?" she cried, not even waiting to hear who answered.

"Gilly, he's not available," Aunt Abby said tartly.

"Look, I don't have time to fool around with you, okay? Put Luke on the phone!" She never shouted at her aunt. Never. But she could feel tears pushing behind her eyes, and she never cried, either. She just needed to hear Luke's voice now, immediately. Awkwardly she added, "I need to talk to him. Please."

"I'll get him," Abby said.

"Gilly? This is Uncle Fitz. Can I help? Your aunt thought—"

"Why can't I talk to Luke?"

"Because he's—" Abruptly Fitz broke off. "Here he is."

"Gilly, what is it?" Luke sounded breathless and strange, as if he'd run a mile to get to the phone. Maybe they'd had to wake him or something. "Is it Nightshade?"

"No, not him. Someone…someone else…broke into my apartment. One of the guys from the alley. Luke, it was awful! He had a knife and he told me to stop being a pest—"

"Slow down. It's okay." His voice was deep and soothing. Gilly reminded herself to breathe in and out, steadily, evenly. "Where are you now? Are you safe?"

"Yes, I think so. I put a dresser in front of the window where he came in. Besides, I don't think he'll be back." She pushed a hand through her hair. "He said he had a message to deliver and that was it."

"And the message was?"

"To stay away from the city council, to stop any campaign against the casino, I guess. He even said to disband the poor NOD Squad and to tell Nightshade to stay away." She was hit with a sudden thought. "Oh, my God! I'll bet this little creep is the one who's been following me! He could even be the one from school the other day. I didn't get a good look. Of course, there could be more than one. There were two in the alley."

"More than one? Someone's been following you?" Luke's voice was rising. "Why the hell didn't you tell me this stuff?"

"Why would I tell you?" she asked, baffled. "It would have just worried you, and what could you have done, anyway? You've been sick in bed, right?"

"Sort of," he muttered, and she could tell he felt guilty about being ill when she needed him. Although it was selfish and petty, it gave her a warm feeling to know that Luke was beating himself up about that.

"It doesn't matter how many of them there are," she declared. "I'm not backing down. I am not turning my neighborhood over to bullies like that."

"Good for you," Luke said softly. "And I'll be right there with you."

Gilly's heart skipped a beat. It really sounded as if he cared. And when she remembered the kiss they'd shared at the museum, she could almost believe there was something magic happening between the two of them after all this time.

Her gaze caught the dresser wedged in front of the window, and she had to rethink her magic theory. After all, she'd had a few too many visitors tonight, and at least one of them put a serious crimp in any rosy thoughts about Luke.

He went on, saying sweet, soothing words. But would he be this sweet if she filled him in on the way she had just behaved with Nightshade? She was beginning to feel more than a twinge of guilt about that, and not just for being a general-purpose wanton.

It was very strange, but in her heart of hearts, chatting so amiably with Luke this way, she felt false and faithless. As if she'd been cheating on him with Nightshade.

She knew very well she hadn't cheated on Luke. Of course not! They were just friends. Always friends. Best of friends.

So why did she feel this incredible guilt? And why did she want Luke to run right over and put his arms around her and blot out any inkling of a memory of Nightshade?

You are treading on dangerous ground here, she

warned herself. Luke, Nightshade, one or the other, either or neither. Dangerous ground.

In the background she could hear Aunt Abby squawking in protest, making pretty much the same point to Luke about her. She distinctly heard her aunt shout, ''What can you be thinking?'' But Luke shushed her.

''Gilly, just tell me where and when you want me, and I'll be there,'' he said firmly.

Where and when she wanted him? Gilly swallowed, her eyes catching the rumpled bed. How about right here and right now?

But she had a feeling that wasn't what he had in mind. Or maybe it was. She wasn't exactly an expert in such matters. Why did sex have to rear its confusing head and make such a hash of things?

''Gilly?'' he prompted. ''Career Day? The Snow Ball? What?''

She brought herself back to earth. Of course, he meant logical, meaningful activities. Go team, rah rah rah.

''Are you sure?'' she asked slowly. ''You want to be on the team all the way?''

''I don't have a choice,'' he said lightly. ''Someone a bit more reliable than your pal Nightshade needs to look after you.''

Well, that was true, wasn't it? Not that Luke had been all that reliable himself lately, but if he was planning to take a firmer stand... The warm feeling expanded to a hum of contentment. Somehow things always seemed brighter when she and Luke worked together.

''So listen, sign me up for Career Day, okay? We'll work out the details later.''

"And the Snow Ball? And maybe a press conference?" she added eagerly.

"Don't push it."

"Luke, that's what I do." Sinking to the floor with the phone to her ear, she smiled. "Pushing it—that's what I do."

"Yeah," he said, "I know. And it's actually starting to be endearing."

It was the nicest thing she'd ever heard.

STILL BUNDLED in the coat, Luke angrily threw his fedora on the table. He'd barely had time to take off his gloves before he'd had to run in the door and take her phone call. But it would hardly do to say, *Sorry I was late getting to the phone. I was just down at your place trying to get your hot little hands off my body before I did something we'd both regret.*

"I am in this up to my neck," he muttered.

"I'll say!" Fitz exclaimed.

Wordlessly Abigail Fitzhugh offered an arm as Luke divested himself of the coat and the hat and the gloves, piece by piece.

"Put this stuff in the trunk of the Ferrari," he ordered, negligently hanging on to the scarf. He stroked it absently. "Given Gilly's current lifestyle, you never know when I might need it again."

Mrs. Fitz stood there, looking down at the armload of clothing. "You can't be serious."

"Perfectly serious."

"Have you thought of retiring this ridiculous Nightshade creature?" Mrs. Fitz demanded. "Of telling Gillian the truth?"

"How could I? After tonight, if she knew the truth, she'd kill me."

Abigail quirked an eyebrow, but he didn't elaborate. He wasn't touching that one.

"So your appearance as Nightshade did not do all you hoped?" Fitz inquired discreetly.

"A lot less than I hoped." Luke couldn't forget Gilly lying half-dressed on the bed, wrapped in his arms, her breasts tantalizing his hands. "And a lot more."

"That doesn't sound promising."

"Not very."

"So now you're signed up for more duty when you know it puts you at considerable risk?" Mrs. Fitzhugh asked.

"That about sums it up."

She heaved a huge sigh and stomped out of the room carrying most of his Nightshade outfit. He could've sworn he heard her growl, "Men!" on her way out.

"Okay, everyone, we're going to be good, right? On our best behavior?" The children nodded dutifully, which was a miracle in itself. "Mr. Blackthorn has been ill, so he may not be really cheery or talkative, but he went to Benny's, just like all of you, and he's a real hero."

She was so nervous on Luke's behalf she was starting to babble. "So he's going to talk to us today about photography. That's what he does—takes pictures. Some of them very famous pictures. You remember we looked at some of his pictures back in the classroom?"

Again they nodded. But they were looking pretty bored.

Don't be bored. Not for Luke, she pleaded. *Be ex-*

cited and cute and adorable so he'll know he's doing the right thing.

But that was a tall order for fourth graders. As they shuffled into Blackthorn Manor in a ragged little line, Gilly wondered again whether she was doing the right thing taking Career Day on the road.

But Luke had preferred doing this on his own turf, plus it would make a great photo opportunity when and if the press arrived. The big hero from the Cretan cave-in, sharing milk and cookies and war stories with kids from her school...

It would be great publicity for Benny's, spark some interest in the campaign to save the school and tie it firmly in the public's mind to its most famous alumnus.

A perfect plan. Except for one little wrinkle. She wasn't at all sure Luke was in full possession of his faculties. If he was going to go running for the hills the first time something spooked him, they were all in trouble. Instead of Hero Alum, they would be publicizing Nutcase Alum. Not really what she had in mind.

"Luke is no nutcase," she told herself sternly. "Not my Luke."

"What did you say, Ms. Quinn?"

"Nothing, sweetie. Nothing."

She ushered the children into the big formal living room, which looked as if it hadn't seen visitors in years, as if the dust covers had only moments before been whipped off the Louis XIV sofa and chairs.

The drapes were a subdued silver blue, the carpet plush and very white. After twenty-five fourth graders tramped over it, it would be gray like the rest of the house, she mused.

The only other adornment were his photos, blown

up and set around the room on easels, the better to showcase his career. Gilly smiled. That had been her idea.

Aunt Abigail entered with cookies and punch for the kids, which gave Gilly another momentary heart attack. Red punch? On white carpet?

She forced herself to relax. Who cared if there were footprints or spots on the rug? That was life, after all— messy, dirty, fun, invigorating. If it had to be cleaned up afterward, so be it.

And then Luke walked in. He was a little pale, but very handsome in a white shirt open at the neck, dark trousers, dark jacket. He didn't rush to hug or kiss her, and she didn't make a move either, suddenly a little shy with her dearest friend.

She could see it in his eyes—he was trying to be strong and brave when he really wasn't sure he was up to entertaining twenty-five nine-year-olds.

"Hi," he mouthed across the room.

"Hi, yourself." With a smile of encouragement, she announced, "Children, this is Mr. Blackthorn."

"Call me Luke."

The kids regarded him uneasily, clutching their paper cups of punch and staring around the formal room with its fancy furnishings.

"We have half an hour with Luke's undivided attention before the reporters come," Gilly said, then prodded. "You all brought questions for Luke, right?"

"I did, I did!" exclaimed Samantha Dunwoody, an unusually self-possessed child. "Why do you take so many gray pictures and not colored ones?"

"And what about a camcorder? Do you have a camcorder? We have a camcorder," chimed in Kendra, Samantha's best friend.

The ice was broken. Gilly hung back, letting Luke lead. He was a little distant, a little protective, but very kind and charming. He showed them his favorite camera, talked about his photos, answered the same questions several times and let each child take a picture or two.

He was warming up, she could tell, and a sparkle seemed to return to his eyes as he began to snap pictures of the children himself. He was just lining them up for a group photo when the first of the reporters arrived.

Gilly started to warn Luke, but the reporter caught her arm. "No, this is great. Let him go."

Luke turned, instantly aware of the media presence. He glanced over, but went back to his photography as one and then another reporter filed in. Gilly wasn't surprised to see Devon Drake in the pack, giving up on her search for Nightshade long enough to cover the return of a local hero.

"Hey, Luke!" Kendra called out, squirming on the couch, front and center in the posed photo. "Do you have that one picture of the bull? We all saw that. But it's not here with all these big poster ones."

"Actually no, I don't," he murmured.

"I do!" Samantha cried, lurching forward just as he clicked the shutter. "I cut it out of the paper. I love that picture! I brought it so I could get your autograph. Can I get your autograph, Luke? I have Frank Thomas and Harold Baines at home. Do you know Frank Thomas and Harold Baines? Have you ever taken their picture?"

"No, I've never met them." He stood, tensing, as the little girl shoved a piece of newspaper at him.

His picture of the bull.

Gilly watched nervously, keeping one eye on Luke, one eye on the phalanx of reporters. What would he do? Would he wig out like he had at the Minoan exhibit?

He held the newspaper clipping in his hand and stared down at it for long moments. Finally, when Gilly had just about fainted with the rising tension, he said, "Pretty good picture, isn't it?"

"I like it," Samantha agreed. "I like bulls."

Swiftly Luke signed his name across the bottom of the paper and handed it back to the girl. But intrepid little Sam wasn't finished yet.

"How did you get out when you were stuck in the cave?" she persisted. "Did you see the Minotaur?"

"They, uh, learned about the Minotaur in mythology last week," Gilly explained.

"I bet you left a trail of bread crumbs, right?" Kendra piped up, not wanting to be outdone by her friend.

Gilly could read the discomfort on his face. He'd never even discussed his sojourn in the labyrinth with her, let alone a roomful of kids and reporters. Moving fast, she interceded with, "That's enough for today, kids. Luke has been really nice—"

"No, no, we want to know!" they chorused. Sam started jumping up and down with excess energy.

"C'mon, Luke, answer the kids," a reporter in thick black glasses said impatiently. "Everyone wants to know. How did you get out of that place?"

There was a long pause. Gilly didn't know what to do. Should she rescue him? Or let it go?

You decide, she thought, sending him a telepathic message. *It's up to you.*

Luke bent down to Sam's level and took back the clipping. He gave it another good look and then began,

"It was very dark and very quiet. I didn't know what to do."

"Were you scared?"

"Yeah, I was really scared. I didn't know if there was a way out." His voice was deep and melodic, as if he were telling a fairy tale, and the children were rapt. "I don't know if any of you have ever been stuck in a closet, or maybe just in your room after the lights went out. The dark can be pretty scary."

Wide-eyed, the children nodded quickly.

"But I remembered where the painting of the bull was. And it was like there was someone with me, and I wasn't as scared anymore," he told them softly. "I knew there was very powerful magic there, because the painting was very old and somebody who knew a lot about magic had put it there."

"Like a wizard?" one of the boys asked.

"Merlin?" Kendra tried.

His lips curved into a smile. "Someone like that."

"So what did you do then?"

"Sometimes, when you concentrate really hard, when you try your hardest," he said, "even if it's very dark and you're all alone, you can still find a way if you just remember that the magic is there to help you."

"Like Tinker Bell!" Kendra interrupted, knocking Luke's leg with her fist in excitement.

Luke's smile was so sweet it made Gilly weak in the knees just to see it. "Kind of like Tinker Bell. So that's what I did. I concentrated, I gathered my strength and I found a way. One step at a time. It was very hard and very dark, but I found a way."

"Great story," Devon Drake said, scribbling to get it all down.

"I think that's it for today, kids," Gilly announced, and this time she wasn't allowing any objections. She rounded them up and made them sit still long enough for the reporters to get pictures, and then she turned to Luke. "Did you have anything you wanted to say before we let you get back to your, uh, work?"

"Luke, listen, we have a million questions," a reporter interjected. "How did you really get out? What was all that about magic?"

"I'm not taking any questions," Luke returned carefully. "I have nothing to say about my getting out except what you just heard. As far as I'm concerned, it's all in the past, and I'm looking toward the future now. And by the way, for the record, I hope that future includes the continued good health of the Benedict Academy, where I myself spent some very good years."

"How long have you been back in town?" someone shouted.

"What have you been doing all this time?" another one yelled, raising his voice to be heard over the first one. Gilly winced, remembering how sensitive Luke was to loud voices.

But he just ignored the reporter. "I plan to be very active in the fight to save the West Riverside neighborhood, and especially Benny's Academy. I hope you will all print that at the top of your stories."

"What about the labyrinth? Any lasting effects?"

"No more questions," Gilly declared, stepping in front of him. "You heard what he had to say. Lucas Blackthorn is back, and he's back to help us save the Benedict Academy. Once again he is acting like a hero, don't you agree?"

Aunt Abigail and Uncle Fitz shooed the reporters

out, but they kept firing questions all the way, paying no attention to the fact that no one was answering.

Gilly looked at Luke. "You're not going to get a moment's peace here now," she noted regretfully. "You were right. And I should have known it would happen."

He shrugged. "It would've happened sooner or later, anyway. I knew they'd figure out where I was as soon as they really tried." Mischief lit his blue eyes. "I did pretty well, didn't I?"

For a moment it was as if the two of them were all alone, even though the room was full of exuberant children. "Luke, you were fabulous." She knew her own eyes were shining with pride and joy and...love. She didn't care.

Stretching up on tiptoe, she kissed him on the cheek, warmly pressing her lips to that sculpted jaw.

Luke hesitated a second, and then, to her surprise, he laughed out loud.

"Thank you," he said as if she had just given him his very own signed copy of the *Mona Lisa*. "I feel great. Do you believe it? I feel great."

"Of course I believe it."

But as she shepherded the students back outside to the bus, she couldn't help wondering why he was so shocked.

Chapter Twelve

"I feel great," he insisted as Abigail frowned. "We've gone over it and over it, and that's all I can tell you— I feel great."

"You had earplugs."

"Yes, I did."

"It was very short-term. And we controlled the lighting."

"Yes, we did." He smiled recklessly. "So what? Don't you see? There were people and noise and questions and that little girl pounded me on the knee and Gilly kissed my cheek, and through it all, I felt great."

"It's nothing you can depend on," she maintained.

He shook his head. "You don't understand. I was right the first time. The meditation and the sensory-deprivation tank, plus some extra sleep—it really works. I can control it."

"You don't know that. This Snow Ball thing is completely different."

"Abby," he chided, shocking her by dropping a kiss on the top of her head, "don't you see? For the first time I have real hope."

"Oh, Lucas..." His housekeeper sounded soft and motherly. "I just don't want you to get your hopes up and then get hurt. We don't know enough about this…thing. What if something really goes wrong and we can't fix it? What if we can't fix *you?*''

''I feel great,'' he repeated with a careless shrug. ''A few phone calls, a meeting or two with a politician just to remind them what the Blackthorn name has always meant in this town—I've done it all over the past few days, and it was a breeze. Gilly really thinks the tide is turning in our favor.''

He didn't tell Abigail that he had also carefully refrained from any prolonged contact with Gilly. He knew he was afraid to be alone with her, afraid of what would surely happen. *Chicken.* But as long as he didn't blow any circuits, he could pretend that it wasn't going to happen again.

It isn't going to happen again, he told himself. *I'm much better.* And if he could make it true by sheer strength of will, it would be so.

Tonight. The Snow Ball. The big gala to show off the school to every bigwig in town. He had pulled in a few old political favors left by his father and his grandfather, but he had helped Gilly make the Snow Ball into what she wanted. He would be there, dressed up like a penguin, willing to dance for perhaps the first time in his adult life just to make the evening perfect.

And tonight, after this final test, if he was still feeling well, he planned to make his move.

He planned to make love to Gilly.

And then he would tell her about his strange powers, about Nightshade, everything.

''You're riding for a fall, Luke.''

He fiddled with the knot on his tie. He was practically pain-free, if it hadn't been for the damn tie.

"Stop being such a ray of sunshine, will you? And Abby—you and Fitz need to get on the road if you're going to make it to Springfield by midnight. You have to be at that antique fair first thing in the morning, or the Chippendale table I want will be gone."

Her frown was etched deep in her narrow face. "We don't have to go tonight. There'll be other Chippendale tables."

"We've been through this. I want *that* table. It's exactly like the one that used to be in the front hall."

It was just a ruse, and he figured they probably both knew that. But if his life was going to take a great turn tonight—or even if it was going to shatter into bits—he'd rather they were out of sight when it happened. He wanted neither congratulations nor I-told-you-so's from his household staff. And even if they didn't want to go, they couldn't refuse a direct order. In many ways he might be their charge, even their child, but he was their boss, too.

"Go," he commanded. "Have fun."

As she hesitated, Luke glanced at his watch. In another sign of progress, for the first time since the accident he could wear a watch without the incessant ticking driving him nuts.

"I'm already late," he noted. "Gilly is probably biting her nails wondering if I'm going to show at all."

Abigail fixed him with one last disapproving look. "Be careful," she said, and then she finally consented to leave him alone with his tie and his watch and his jumpy nerves.

GILLY WAS IN HEAVEN. Well, at least as close as she could be without Luke. Where was he? She craned her neck, scanned the crowd, but he wasn't there.

The music, the flowers, the steady stream of donations to the Save Benny's fund—it was all going very well indeed.

But where was Luke? He wouldn't punk out on her tonight of all nights, surely? He'd been so terrific the past few days, calling people, haranguing the mayor, taking on just about anything she asked.

Of course, she hadn't seen much of him herself. But all that would change tonight.

She was wearing a white dress she had borrowed from Suzette, who had a much better wardrobe than she did. It was not her usual style, with its short, frothy skirt and fitted bodice, and she had occasional moments when she looked down and felt like an impostor. Still, it was a beautiful dress, and several of her students had been shocked to see her in something other than her usual jeans, T-shirt and blazer. She wasn't sure anyone at school had ever seen her legs! Especially not in heels, which made them look longer and all the more unfamiliar.

"Wow, Ms. Q!" Even cooler-than-a-cucumber Tony was impressed.

"Yeah, yeah, I know." She smiled at him, still feeling awkward. All this attention was fun, but awfully strange.

"Is that him? The hero?" a nearby society matron whispered loudly. And then Gilly heard the rush of whispers, the oohs and ahhs, and she knew Luke had arrived.

"Finally," she breathed, making her way as quickly

as she could through the crowd. She wanted to get to him before the mayor or some other hot dog nabbed him.

He was standing just inside the door to the school gym, underneath the big paper snowflake they'd hung as a decoration. His hair was still too long, but it framed his elegant face beautifully, and he was wearing a white dinner jacket with black tie and black trousers. He had one hand in his pocket as he stood there, lazy, casual, gazing around at the crowd, a funny half-smile playing about his narrow, sexy lips.

And then he saw her. His smile widened. His hot blue gaze swept over her, from head to toe, brushing and teasing her with its flames.

And Gilly's breath was gone, knocked right out of her.

Everybody there looked pretty spiffy tonight, but nobody held a candle to Luke. And the way he was looking at her. Only her.

"Hi," she murmured, feeling like an idiot for not having anything better to say. "You look...delicious."

He laughed. But she was completely serious.

"You look delicious, too." He took her hand, leading her skillfully through the crowd, finding the most shadowy corner. And then he pulled her hard into his arms, faking a step or two, making it look vaguely as though they were dancing when all she was doing was holding on for dear life.

His arms tightened. "I like the dress," he murmured in her ear. "Kind of like whipped cream." And then he pulled her even closer, touching just the tip of his tongue to her ear. "Whipped cream. So...lickable."

Her heart dropped to her knees. Luke, making naughty small talk? What twilight zone was this?

You know what? she answered herself. *I don't care. Tonight is tonight, and that's good enough.*

When she was sixteen, she'd prayed every night to St. Anthony, patron saint of lost causes, to make Luke look at her this way, just once. Okay, so a few years had passed, and neither of them was really the same person. She'd given up on St. Anthony—and on men—a long time ago.

But here they were, and he wasn't just looking at her—his eyes were devouring her. No way was she going to let this opportunity slide.

She could see the gleam of amusement, of desire, in his gaze, but she closed her own eyes and nestled closer, vainly listening for the music to guide her. All she could hear was his racing heartbeat. He was lean, hot, his body thrumming with tension under her fingers.

His lips were so close; it was only an extra fraction of an inch to edge nearer, to lift her mouth to his. The kiss was soft, forgiving, gentle at first. But soon he stopped any pretense of dancing, framing her face with his long, clever fingers. He deepened the kiss, drawing her in, exploring her lips, serving plenty of hard, inescapable notice that there was more behind this kiss than mere friendship.

Gilly felt as if she were falling under a spell. She couldn't pull away, could only kiss him back with every ounce of passion and joy she felt racing through her veins.

It was the same as the kiss in the museum, and yet so different, too—not as rushed, not as frantic, even more dazzling. And yet familiar in a strange way—

"Ahem." A woman cleared her throat expressively. "Excuse me, you two, but this is a school function. No making out, please."

Aflame with embarrassment, still dizzy and tingling, Gilly broke away from Luke and wheeled around to face her punishment. "Suzette. Hello." She saw that her friend's eyes were sparkling with merriment, but it didn't help. Luke moved securely behind her, very close, very solid, as if protecting her. That helped a little.

"You want me to have to get out the ruler to separate you two?"

"That won't be necessary," Luke promised, straight-faced. Gilly could feel that he had tucked up her skirt just a little in the back and was tickling her thigh. She bit her lip, but his fingers continued their insidious path.

"Luke," she tried, her voice coming out unnaturally high. "Can you behave yourself, please?"

"Looked to me like neither of you were doing too well there," Suzette interjected. "Never happened when *I* wore that dress, I'll tell you."

"I'm sure it's lovely on you, too," Luke said politely, but his hand was creeping up to where it should not have been. There was nothing but a wall behind them, so no one could tell that he was taking liberties with the curve of her bottom under the flouncy skirt. But Gilly could certainly tell. And when he hit the lacy line of her panties, she let out a tiny squeak of protest.

"I don't know what's going on with you," Suzette said suspiciously. "But whatever it is, just don't be too obvious, okay? We're trying to show off how moral and high-toned we are. Hanky-panky," she added, casting a jaded eye at Gilly's rising color and Luke's studied innocence, "is not on the bill."

"Got it," Gilly returned quickly, trying to maintain her composure as little flicks of fire quite literally reached up and pinched her in the behind.

"Got it," Luke chorused. The swine.

As soon as Suzette was a few feet away, Gilly slapped away his hand and smoothed her skirt. "Luke, that was terrible!"

"I'm sorry," he said soothingly. "I couldn't help myself. It's that skirt."

"Oh, it is not. You're just being wicked tonight."

"And you love it."

His smile was incorrigible. "Yes," she said, laughing, tipping into his chest so he would put his arms around her again. "I do love it."

Her words were almost drowned out by a sudden disturbance behind them. Someone yelled, "Fight!" and there was a shuffle of feet and bodies. Gilly could hear the crack of flesh hitting flesh, a girl screaming, "No!" and one of the older students—a senior perhaps—went down like a sack of potatoes, narrowly missing toppling the refreshment table.

Lena Winslow, the Latin teacher, had been manning the table, and she leaped back, clasping the whole punch bowl to her chest to secure it.

Another kid—someone Gilly didn't recognize— shouted, "Keep your hands off my woman!" The kid lunged in the direction of the boy on the floor, who was holding a hand to a newly bloodied nose. More teenagers rushed in, taking sides in the dispute.

Suzette made a beeline for the center of the disturbance. Gilly, headed that way, too, weaving through students, parents, politicians and a minister or two, all of whom were shuffling their feet uneasily and watching the fight.

Gilly reached the boy on the floor first, while Suzette cornered the other combatant. "I didn't touch his girlfriend," the boy with the bloody nose told Gilly sulkily. "Jerk came out of nowhere."

"Well, that's okay. Nobody's hurt." She helped dust him off and found him a handkerchief for his nose. She was just turning to tell the milling crowd that order had been restored when all hell broke loose again.

A wealthy woman in a tight cocktail dress suddenly yelped, smacking someone with her tiny evening purse as a man on the opposite side of the gym hollered, "Pickpocket! That kid stole my wallet!"

"My necklace!" screamed another woman. "There are thieves everywhere! The place is crawling with them!"

People began to push and shove, plowing under anyone in the way. The man who'd lost his wallet elbowed someone else out of the way, apparently trying to pursue his chief suspect, but the guy he shoved didn't appreciate it any and swung out with a fist. He missed his target, but he did connect soundly with the mayor's wife's face.

The poor woman began shrieking, "By dose! By dose!" which Gilly took to mean that they'd suffered another nasal casualty.

"Everybody just calm down!" she shouted, but panic had already set in. Everywhere people were scrambling for the exits. Lena Winslow, however, was still bravely clutching the punch bowl.

The mayor was nowhere to be seen—presumably he'd escaped at the first whiff of trouble—but his chief aide was sitting on the floor by his boss's wife, pressing his hankie to her nose, looking white as a sheet. All the other VIPs were lost in the sea of screaming flailing humanity.

The Snow Ball was an unmitigated disaster.

Gilly realized belatedly that she had lost Luke. There was no way to find him now, not with so much chaos surrounding her. Oh, God. Luke. Smack-dab in the middle of all this noise and confusion when he was still a bit shaky just being out in public. This must be driving him crazy. Gilly scanned the ballroom desperately. *What was happening to Luke?*

"I have to find him," she said, but there was just no way. She almost considered getting down on her hands and knees and crawling through the sea of legs, but she knew she'd never make it.

"Look on the bright side," she whispered as the refreshment table collapsed under the weight of two middle-aged politicians engaged in fisticuffs, and six platters' worth of cupcakes and Rice Krispie squares went sailing into the crowd. "Things couldn't get any worse."

She knew immediately she shouldn't have said that. First somebody collided with poor Lena Winslow, and the punch bowl was history. The mayor's wife had just started to rise to her feet when the tide of Tahitian-pink liquid sloshed her way, and down she went like the *Titanic*.

And then the lights went out.

Gilly stayed where she was, and she hoped everybody else did the same thing. But there was too much movement around her for her to feel that optimistic. She was elbowed one way, jostled the other, and then a very fresh hand closed over one breast. She grabbed the hand, yanked the guy closer and kicked him, hard.

"That'll teach you to grope me!"

A light went on in the hallway outside the gym, and somebody turned on a flashlight, which gave the room an eerie glow. A roar seemed to go up on the side by the big field-house doors, and cold air rushed in. The street lamps outside cast a few murky rays in through the now open doors, but not enough for anyone to really see anything. Still, the crowd seemed to have taken up some kind of anthem. What were they saying, all run together and jumbled like that?

"Nightshade?" Gilly echoed, stunned down to her uncomfortable high heels. "I forgot all about him."

Clearly he hadn't forgotten about her. If she squinted, she thought she could see his dark broad-shouldered form and the rakish cast of his fedora silhouetted against the open gym doors. The sea of people seemed to part for him, fights broke off in midpunch, and the noise level subsided immediately.

She never had figured out how his mere presence seemed so daunting before he even moved a muscle. But whatever magic he wielded, it was working tonight. There was a slam and a thunk, a gasp. Everyone in the gym seemed to be holding his or her breath.

Gilly saw the black-cloaked figure striding closer. *He's coming for me,* she thought, hope rising in her heart. In spite of her best intentions, she was filled with the same sizzling passion he always provoked, the same incredibly heightened awareness of his big solid body.

"Nightshade," she breathed, reaching out as the man in the black hat moved closer.

He swept right past her without so much as a hello.

A second later he came slashing back through the crowd, dragging someone by the neck. And then he was gone.

The power was restored and the overhead lamps flooded the field house. Everyone seemed to blink in unison and stare at one another and the debris. From outside, sirens fractured the night, announcing the arrival of the police. The commissioner and the mayor had been in attendance tonight, and it still took the authorities a good half hour to respond to an emergency in West Riverside.

But Nightshade was nowhere to be seen.

Gilly was curiously deflated. She should've been happy the melee was over, furious that her Snow Ball was decimated, desolate that her plan to show off Benny's was in tatters. But all she could think about was how Nightshade had ignored her. She might as well have been one of the folding chairs, for all the attention he'd paid her.

She felt a tug on her arm. "Ms. Quinn?" It was Javier, one of her art students. "There's this guy who sent me to get you. Mr. Blackthorn?"

"Luke?" Holy hell, she'd forgotten all about him!

Javier ducked back into the crowd, leading her outside through the gym doors. A cold wind whipped around her, and she felt instantly chilled.

Shivering, she asked, "He's out here?"

"Yeah, Ms. Q," Javier responded. "Right over here."

The police were just entering that way, so things were a bit confused. The mayor and his pal Ed Spivak, who had argued on behalf of the casino to the city council, were hobnobbing off to one side, smoking cigars, looking very unconcerned, which made Gilly's blood boil. How dare they not even care that her Snow Ball had been smashed into smithereens?

She passed by smartly, her chin in the air. Next, Gilly and Javier made their way around a pile of bodies—not dead ones, just injured. There were four of them, all tied up in a neat bundle. They might as well have been marked Culprits they looked so guilty.

"Nightshade asked me to keep watch over them," a round, red-faced man announced proudly. "I guess they're like a band of pickpockets or something. He rounded them up and dropped them here."

A cop tipped back his hat and scratched his head. "So how did Nightshade know these were the right guys?"

"Beats me," their temporary guard said. "Might want to take a look in their pockets, though." He pointed to a bright diamond necklace trailing out of one coat pocket, and a nice little haul of billfolds peeking out of another.

Good old Nightshade, always rushing to the rescue. Well, bully for him. Why couldn't he have stopped the thieves *before* they ruined her party? And why couldn't he have at least stopped to say hello?

Thinking about Nightshade when she should've been thinking about Luke only made her feel guilty. She picked her way past the thugs as best she could, still following Javier's lead. Around the back, on the gym steps, she finally saw Luke. "Oh, God," she said. "You look terrible."

His clothes were a mess, and he looked drawn, bruised and shell-shocked. She ran to his side, cradled his head in her hands, kissed his face. "I'm so sorry! What happened? Did someone hit you? If it was that Nightshade, I swear I'll kill him. He must've passed right by here. Oh, Luke, you didn't try to help him, did you?''

She glanced over at the moaning pile of thugs. "Luke, you didn't get involved! Tell me you didn't! Nightshade may be Mr. Crimefighter Extraordinaire, but you're just a regular guy." She felt like wringing her hands or at least stamping her foot. "Oh, Luke, this is awful. And it's all my fault! I'm so sorry."

"Not your fault," he muttered, tensing and wincing as he forced himself to sit up straight, sending her a dark look that shouted how much he did *not* want to be coddled.

"Not my fault?" Gilly wasn't as forgiving. She braced him against her shoulder to try to help him to his feet. "I brought—no, make that, I pushed—an emotionally fragile, possibly agoraphobic man into a madhouse! So whose fault is it?"

He edged away. "Gilly, I came under my own steam. I'm not emotionally fragile. And I'm certainly not agoraphobic."

"Whatever you say." But it didn't stop the panic and the tenderness from seeping out all over her. She never should've let Luke come to this, never should've pushed him to recover too fast. "Luke, there are ambulances here. I think we should get a doctor or paramedic to—"

"No doctors," he growled.

"Okay, well, I really think we should get you home, then. Bed rest is probably the best thing."

"Bed rest?" He stood, stiff and wobbly at the same time, his jaw clenched so tight she thought it might crack. "Not exactly what I had planned for tonight."

"Well, you know, plans change. Get over it."

She hadn't meant to snap at him, but she hated it

when he got moody and cranky. Suddenly she remembered whose fault this whole mess was, and she relented immediately. She reached out a hand to stroke his cheek, wishing he didn't flinch as her fingers grazed his skin.

"Luke, I think you should go home. Doesn't that sound like the best thing right now?"

He nodded. And then, with a fierce look of determination, he put one foot in front of the other and strode for the Ferrari. Gilly sort of hovered behind him, ready to help if she needed to, fully aware he would rather die than let her.

He reached into his pocket and retrieved his keys, tossing them to her with studied carelessness. "You drive," he muttered.

"Looks like maybe your car was robbed, too." She pointed to the trunk lid, which was slightly ajar. "Should I check to see if anything is missing?"

"No," he said abruptly. He used whatever strength he had to reach over and slam it shut, but she could see the effort it cost him.

"Come on, get in." She bundled him into the passenger seat and then went around to the driver's side. And then she took a deep breath and stared down at the stick shift, praying she could drive the car well enough to get them back to Blackthorn Manor.

"Thank God Aunt Abby and Uncle Fitz are gone for the weekend. They'd kill me for this," she mumbled. "And they'd be justified if they did. Maybe I'll just kill myself and get it over with."

"Don't be so hard on yourself," Luke murmured. He leaned back his head, gritting his teeth as the car lurched down the street. Then he closed his eyes and seemed to drift away, into sleep or unconsciousness or something.

Gilly's heart beat faster. "Are you with me, Luke? Are you okay?" But he didn't answer.

She ignored a stop sign on the empty street, accelerating, heading for the bridge as fast as she could, determined not to shift again and risk killing the engine. She spared him an anxious glance. "You'll be all right, Luke. I promise."

Why wasn't he moving? Why didn't he respond, even with a moan or a groan?

"You have to be okay, Luke," she whispered. "You have to be. I lo—"

She broke off, unwilling to finish that last devastating word. But it echoed large and loud in her heart.

I love you.

Chapter Thirteen

"Gilly," Luke said clearly, "if you could possibly avoid at least one pothole, I would appreciate it."

She laughed out loud. Trust Luke to burst that bubble. Here she was, thinking he'd breathed his last and broken her heart both at the same time, and he was just cranky about potholes.

"You sound like your old self," she said happily, turning off the bridge and onto the private road that ran in front of the big houses on the bluff.

But the words *I love you* still hovered in the intimate space of the car, and she couldn't get them out of her mind.

Of course I love him. I've always loved him.

But that was different. She'd loved him as in impossible crush on a dangerous boy who made movie stars seem tame. She'd loved him as a dear friend, someone whose distance made him even dearer.

But now...now she was filled with this incredible warmth and joy and longing. She wanted to make love to him. She wanted him to hold her and fuss over her. And make love to her. Definitely make love to her.

But actually wanting someone to take care of her was a pretty odd feeling. She was the one always run-

ning to fix it, mend it, jump-start it, finish it, whatever
it was. How would it feel to have someone like Luke
pamper and spoil her, even for just a little while? How
would it feel to have him bring her breakfast in bed,
draw her a bath, ply her with champagne?

She imagined sharing the bath, pouring the champagne on his hard-muscled chest and licking it off. If
she hadn't been driving, if he hadn't been broken and
battered, she would've pulled over and ravaged him
right then, with or without champagne.

As she pulled into Blackthorn Manor's long driveway, she glanced over at Luke and smiled mistily. He
was very still. His eyes were closed and his jaw was
clenched, as if he was conserving his energy.

Yes, it definitely looked like lust would have to be
postponed for a while. Right now this bright shiny
love, this hope and promise, were what warmed her.
His lashes were dark and thick against his cheeks, and
her heart seemed to expand to hold these new, pre-
cious feelings.

She loved Luke. Wow.

HE OPENED HIS EYES a crack, trying not to process the
whole litany of small and large agonies his brain was
frantically relaying.

Why was Gilly staring at him that way? Wasn't it
bad enough that she was treating him like a small boy
who'd cracked up his bike? The torment of watching
that tremulous concern, that outrageous outpouring of
sympathy, was far worse than any physical pain he'd
endured.

Sympathy was not what he wanted from Gilly.

Especially not now, not when he'd planned to carry

her home from the Snow Ball and sweep her off her feet. And into his bed.

Yeah, right. A man who couldn't walk a straight line without lurching from the exertion, a man who had no pretty words, no sensual weapons, nothing but a major case of guilt to work with, had about as much chance of a seduction scene as he did of climbing Mount Everest in swim fins.

He sent Gilly a searching glance. What was she thinking? What was she doing here when they both knew she'd rather be with that damn Nightshade? *She is with that damn Nightshade. But she doesn't know it.*

How could he ever have thought for one second he could pull this off? Arrogance. Pride. Stupidity.

He cursed himself. He'd created Nightshade to save her skin. How could he have known he would manufacture the perfect rival? Her words still echoed in his too-sensitive ears. *Nightshade may be Mr. Crimefighter Extraordinaire, but you're just a regular guy.*

Just a regular guy who couldn't touch the woman he loved.

One lousy kiss had sent him over the edge, and yet somehow he'd deluded himself into thinking he could make love to Gilly with no fallout, no sensory overload. Pretty ironic he hadn't gotten far enough to test his theory. A bit of a fistfight, and he was history.

Suddenly, with terrible conviction, Luke knew he couldn't take any more of this, not one more second of her misty eyes and kind smiles, her innocent concern for his well-being while she mooned over the amazing Nightshade, who fought off whole gangs of thugs without breaking a sweat. If only she knew.

"I'm going in," he said abruptly.

It took him a moment to maneuver himself out the passenger door, accompanied by lots of muttered swearwords. *Oh, yeah.* He was making himself more and more attractive by the minute. Gilly stayed with him, acting her usual cheerful self, which only made things worse.

"Oh, come on," she said, in a teasing tone. "Up the stairs, into bed. It's not so far."

But when they hit the first step, he stumbled. She reached out to catch him, losing her balance, too. They ended up tangled on the landing, with most of her body beneath his. If he'd thought he was too battered to respond to her physically, he was very wrong. All his neurons were firing like champions.

Luke didn't move, didn't dare disrupt this incredible feeling. It felt so innocent, so easy. He opened the sensory gates just a little, absorbing the fresh, heady feel and smell of her skin, taking in the forbidden joy of her soft curves pressed so close. A silky red tendril brushed his hand and sent little flickers of pleasure skating up his arm right to his heart, heightening what had already become more than an ache, more than a twinge. He wanted her desperately. The signals couldn't have been clearer.

"Well," she said breathlessly, "it feels to me like you're all in one piece."

One piece in particular. How inconvenient for his body to respond like a stallion at the gate when he had just decided there was no way, no chance, no—

Was that a moan? It was so soft she couldn't have known she'd done it, but *he* knew. "Oh, God," he whispered. "Don't do this to me."

Then she wiggled almost imperceptibly, and his

need became so overpowering he couldn't think of anything else but stopping it. Now.

"I can't do this," he mumbled, edging away.

But Gilly looped her arms around his chest and nudged him back. "You feel just fine. Mmm. Very fine."

"Gilly, stop it."

Carefully he disengaged himself and staggered the rest of the way upstairs, waving her off as she attempted to support him. He toppled into bed, not bothering to undress. *Control it,* he commanded himself. *You can do it.* But his nerves were still ragged, and his veins flowed with crystal-pure desire and need and...Gilly.

If she didn't get out of here within the next three seconds, he wouldn't be responsible.

"Okay, Gilly, you did your duty. I'm not a child. No need to tuck me in or bring me cocoa or button my jammies," he said, rather more savagely than he'd intended.

"Funny. I never imagined you as the pajama-wearing type." And she had the audacity to wink at him.

He snapped, "This is not a joke, Gilly."

"I know it's not a joke. I know you could've been seriously hurt." She gave him another one of those mushy, compassionate looks and he groaned. "For all I know, you are seriously hurt. Come on, let's look."

Without asking or hesitating, she leaned over him and summarily dragged off his jacket, first one arm and then the other. "Gilly," he protested, but she ignored him.

"You didn't actually tell me what happened. Were you crushed in the mad rush to the door? Or did somebody take a swing at you because you accidentally pinched his wife's behind?''

"Nothing like that," Luke muttered as she took off his tie. "Let's just say I have a low pain threshold."

"The whole thing was really suspicious, if you ask me."

He stiffened. "What?"

"Tonight." She frowned down at him. "Why would a gang of pickpockets right out of *Oliver Twist* decide to crash the Snow Ball? Nothing like that has ever happened before! And why were the mayor and his chum Spivak so darned happy about it?"

She shook her head, still clutching Luke's jacket as she spoke. He could practically see the gears turning in that quick little brain, but he was way ahead of her. At least this was a safe topic, miles away from...the other thing.

"At first I thought the mayor was just exploiting the fact that West Riverside isn't the safest place around," Gilly continued. "But now I think he and his pals were actually behind some of the things that have been happening. Like that little creep who came to visit me. And this rash of thefts and fights at the Snow Ball. Very convenient."

"Very," Luke agreed.

Gilly stood. "I think I should call my old pal Devon Drake and give her the story. I'd love to see our honorable mayor get what's coming to him."

But Luke caught her hand. "There's more."

"What do you mean?"

He smiled grimly. "Sometimes it pays to be in the wrong place at the right time. When I was outside the school, I overheard Spivak telling one of the thugs what a good job they'd done. He paid him off—gave him a couple of hundred bucks. And when the mayor joined him, Spivak told him they should give the kids a tip for a job well-done.''

"Don't you see what that means?" she asked eagerly. "Luke, we have proof! Where's the phone? If we call Devon right now, maybe she can still get it in tomorrow's paper." He lay back, not agreeing, not encouraging, and she stopped short. "Come on, Luke. Don't you want this over with tonight?"

Still holding her hand, Luke drew her closer. He had visions of Devon Drake and her cronies invading his house, of interviews and cameras and press conferences. With Nightshade paraphernalia still in his trunk, with no protection from snoops or sensations. Would anyone believe proof delivered by a freak trembling in the corner, overpowered by bright lights and loud noises?

Sure, he wanted to get the mayor as much as anyone. Just not this moment. Not until he had a chance to think about how best to engineer this. "How about if we call Devon in the morning?" he suggested, not above looking a little shaky on purpose. He knew exactly what Gilly's reaction would be. With a small gasp, a tiny grimace, he said, "I'm really not in the mood tonight."

"Oh, dear. Of course you're not. What was I thinking?" Her eyes swept over him quickly. "I don't see any blood, although you have a bruise on your cheek." She touched it tentatively, and he swore again before he could stop himself. He might've faked the grimace, but when she poked at him like that, the pain was quite real.

After a moment's hesitation she reached over and

neatly popped off his first shirt stud. "Here, let's get your shirt and pants off, and you can get some sleep."

Gilly's small, cool hands peeling off his shirt, sliding over his chest, his shoulders? Gilly's fingers reaching for his pants, rubbing against his hips, his thighs, his...? He wasn't that crazy.

"I am neither a child nor a eunuch," he retorted angrily. "Get your hands off me."

"I am aware that you are neither a child nor a eunuch," she said with dignity. She gazed down at him, and her eyes seemed to rest on the top button of his trousers. Stiffly she added, "Very aware."

That was all it took. What was he, a saint? Not on your life.

He grabbed her hand and reeled her in. She hit the big black bed with a soft plop as he rolled over and trapped her under the hard length of his body. Both of her shoes went flying; he heard them hit the carpet with two short thumps.

Catching her wrists, Luke propped himself up slightly, holding himself far enough back to gaze down into her emerald eyes. Sensation flooded him, and his nerve endings sang with need and desire. He had tried to hold back, tried to tell himself this was impossible, but it just wasn't working.

Not when her body under his felt this good, this right. Not when he could hear and feel every breath she took, every beat of her heart, racing in sync with his own, pumping into his own veins. She was lying so close he could feel the scallops of lace on her panties burning into the inside of his thigh, feel the heat seeping from her skin into his everywhere they connected, along her legs, her hips, her belly.

"Don't move," he breathed.

Holding himself very still, he took a small moment to savor her warmth and softness, to taste the strong current of excitement emanating from her, even the small frisson of fear. Fear? If she only knew what he knew—that this whole thing might blow up in their faces.

But damn it, he wasn't going to believe that could be true. Making love to her couldn't feel this *necessary* if it was going to destroy him.

"Luke? What's wrong?"

Carefully, quickly, he said, "I've been trying not to think about this, Gilly, because Lord knows what will happen. But I can't go back. I can't make this—whatever it is—not happen."

Her eyes were wide and dazed. "I—I don't know what you mean."

There wasn't time to explain it. *I'm a freak with superacute senses and I don't know what making love will do. If I blow up in your arms, just remember it was worth it.*

So he decided to reduce things to their most basic level.

"You and me. Here and now," he said tersely. "I want to make love to you."

He could see her breath catch in her throat. She scrambled to a sitting position to face him more fully, bracketing his jaw with her hands. Gilly's eyes were searching, unsure.

"Luke, I want to. I've never wanted anything more. But I don't want to hurt you. You were ill." She put a hand to his forehead as if testing his temperature. "Are you sure you're okay?"

Damn it. He didn't want her to worry about him.

He wanted her to *want* him, to feel the same kind of uncontrollable fever he did.

"Forget about everything but now," he ordered. He yanked her into his lap, wrapped her legs around his waist and then bent his head to kiss her full on the lips. Clasping her hard against him, he got the reverberation of every tiny tremor that rocked her, and he loved every minute of it. As his tongue delved into her mouth, he heard the tiny moan that escaped her, and he felt the shivers dancing deep within her.

He knew he was being unfair and he didn't care. Roughly he held her hands in front of him, shaking her with his words. "Say yes, Gilly," he commanded. "Let me love you."

"Love me?" Under his fingers, he could feel her pulse racing in her wrists, rocketing so fast he was afraid she might faint on him. But you would never have known it from her wide, joy-filled smile. Gilly, his Gilly, looped her arms around his neck, tightened her knees around his waist and kissed him back with every ounce of enthusiasm and energy she possessed. "Yes," she said clearly. "Oh, yes."

He could read it in her smile and in her eyes. His senses might be better than anyone else's, but they didn't include mind reading. They didn't need to. He knew. Gilly loved him and she trusted him. She always had.

Making love to her would be the most natural, least risky thing he'd ever done. It had to be.

She laughed, a sound so pure and bright it almost hurt his ears, then she wriggled down to drop kisses on his nose, his cheeks, his jaw. She nibbled at his lips and slid her tongue along the edge of his ear. If he felt any twinge of pain, any warning his senses were in danger, he ignored it. He had waited too long and become too greedy to let anything interfere now.

With a surge of power, he realized he felt fine. Wonderful. Strong. Sure. Touching her and drinking her in seemed to be insulating his jagged nerves better than any remedy he'd tried so far.

"I'll have to remember this," he murmured. "If I'm feeling a little edgy, I'll just make love to you for about six hours until my senses are all damped down."

"Mmm," she murmured as he sent a roving hand under her dress to cup her bottom and center her directly on his lap. "You're displaying an awful lot of energy for someone who didn't look so good an hour ago."

"I conserved my strength," he said, sliding his tongue down the slope of her neck.

"Ohhh..." she sighed, hooking her knee around him, angling closer, shivering, sending new sparks of hunger and impatience through him. "You've conserved enough. Time to spend."

"I really love this dress," he said with a wicked grin, skimming his fingers up under it. He sketched circles around the curve of her derriere, under the lace edge of her panties, around to the inside of her thigh, making her gasp with pleasure and surprise. Her moans gave him plenty of pleasure in return. "This little skirt has been driving me insane all night."

"It's driving me pretty insane at the moment, too," she whispered in a shaky voice, catching him around the neck, tugging him back down to her mouth, urging him on faster with her eager kiss, twisting her arms around him, plastering the front of her dress against his chest.

"Slow down," he whispered, holding back just a bit.

He could tell she was eager to get on with this, but then she never had been one to hang back when she knew what she wanted. Well, for once in her life, Gilly was just going to have to be patient and let him set the pace.

And while he was at it, he made sure the pace he set was excruciating, intoxicating, maddening. He teased her mercilessly, barely grazing her neck and her chin with his wet mouth, sliding his hands over the smooth fabric at her waist and her breasts, leaving a trail of sparks, but never staying long enough to put out any fires.

As she fisted her hands around his collar, his fingers covered hers. "What's your rush?" he asked, swallowing her objections with a kiss.

A moment later he abandoned her lips, pressing her hands out to her sides, pushing her back into the soft bed, capturing and pinning her as he continued that paralyzing trail of sweet slick kisses. He licked her breast through the fabric of her dress, biting down on her nipple, smiling in satisfaction when she arched up to meet him, to bring herself closer, nearer, more fully into his mouth.

He was happy to oblige.

It was amazing how her skin felt—hot, slick, pulsating—as he caressed her through the slinky chiffon. The fabric slithered back and forth over her breast almost in counterpoint to his mouth and tongue. She writhed under him, sending him higher and higher.

"I need to touch you," she pleaded, but Luke shook his head.

All around him, he felt and heard and smelled and

tasted Gilly, the sensations dancing so fast he couldn't really take them in. With his hands and mouth on her, with her scent filling his nose, he was swimming in the shocks and aftershocks of his own pleasure. If she so much as crooked one finger on his bare skin, he was afraid he would go over the top.

"Be patient," he whispered. "I'm just getting started."

He breathed the words over the damp chiffon, and her nipples peaked in response, as if they were aching for his touch, his mouth. "Ah, Gilly," he rasped, "I can feel it every time you tremble." Her whole body was shaking, starting deep inside. He smiled again. He loved the feeling of power her response gave him.

"Suzette is going to kill me for what I'm doing to her dress," she said suddenly. "Maybe I should—"

He cut off her words with a kiss, leaving her breathless and dazed. And then, before she had a chance to react, he reached to the neckline of her dress and slashed it right down the middle. The sound of the fabric ripping into shreds and the sight of her bare skin, reacting subtly to the cool night air, was shocking, stirring.

Carelessly Luke tossed the scraps of chiffon aside. "We'll get Suzette a new dress."

He sat back, his eyes raking her, his mouth suddenly dry. If he licked his lips, would it be insulting? But my, oh, my. All she was wearing was a pair of thin panties and a garter belt and stockings.

"Did you do this on purpose to drive me crazy?" he inquired, reaching slowly, delicately, to pop open her garters. The smooth silky skin at the top of her thigh was warm, and he could see the ripple of sensation on her skin as he stroked one finger around the edge of the sheer stocking.

Gilly swallowed, hard. "If you don't like it, I could take it off," she said quickly.

Luke just grinned. "Let me." First one sleek stocking and then the other. That done, he reached under her and stripped off her panties in a motion so fast he could tell it caught her by surprise. His hand moved between them, tweaking her, stroking her, until she pressed into him, aching for release. But Luke held her back.

She moaned, frustrated. "Please, Luke. I can't wait."

"You will wait."

"No," she said tersely, "I won't."

And then she shoved her hands inside his shirt, scattering shirt studs every which way as she pulled the garment off his smooth muscled chest, making room for her hungry hands and mouth.

Luke felt a quick surge of burning electricity, as tiny lights burst in the periphery of his vision, and small indistinct shocks flickered in the depths of his body. He ignored them. Cupping her bottom in his hands, he sat back, pulling her up into his lap again, making her feel the hot throb of his desire underneath her bare skin. Was he breathing? He wasn't sure. Even breathing had become difficult.

But then, nothing was easy anymore. He couldn't move fast enough, touch enough, taste enough.

This time, when her fingers scrambled for the top of his pants, unfastening, searching, he didn't pull back, didn't put on the brakes. He brushed her hands away and took care of the pants himself.

And then it was just the two of them, skin to skin.

He'd never felt anything smoother, hotter, more amazing in his life, as her body fitted itself to the contours of his. Head to toe, perfect fit.

He had no room to think anymore. All he knew were three words.

Pleasure. Exquisite. Gilly.

He had given his heightened senses free rein before, but not let them arch this high. Skating on the edge of something new and powerful, he was scared out of his wits, and yet, it was the most unbelievable and wonderful feeling of his life. Before, he had felt alone with his crazy powers. Now he felt *together,* melded, one.

He kissed her sweetly and deeply, and then he rested his forehead on hers for just a second.

"Now?" he whispered.

"Now." He felt her smile more than saw it. "Make love to me, Luke."

And with one slick thrust, he pushed inside.

The shocks were wild now—stormy, spiky, sensational. "Yes," he managed to rasp. It was heaven, it was madness, and he could feel the vibrations down to his soul.

He couldn't distinguish between sounds and smells and touches anymore, couldn't tell where she started and he stopped. It was all blurring into one major current of heat and light.

"Yes," he said again, holding her tighter, stroking her higher, feeling her shattering climax with every filament in his body. "Gilly, I love you."

"I know," she breathed into his ear. She smiled, holding him closer, taking him deeper.

And then it happened.

With a feeling of joy and love, he made one last

thrust and then toppled into release with a dazzling shower of sparks. But it went on too long. The current, the sensations, were too strong, too many. Electricity zapped through his veins, coursing through his nervous system, pushing him into an explosion of light and scorching heat. Incredible pain shot through him. Gulping for air, he rolled away, trying to figure out what was happening to him.

He couldn't quite form words or put together the fragile pieces. Too numb perhaps? Had he experienced a blowout? He had no idea. He could—gingerly, painfully—move his muscles. But he felt as though his whole body was encased in lead.

When people said mind-blowing, they had no idea. It was as if every generator in the city had been tuned in to his brain in one massive power surge. *What was happening to him?*

More importantly, what was he going to tell Gilly?

She cuddled closer, her eyes closed, as she reached for his hand. She held it to her heart, whispering, "I just have to tell you that I love you, too. I've always loved you. This...this was unbelievable. I never knew anything could feel so intense. But what I feel in my heart is what's really important, Luke. Because I love you with everything I have."

Luke said nothing. His tongue couldn't seem to get around the words. It was frozen. Yet his body was still pulsing with aftershocks, and his brain felt drizzled with trails of sparks.

She half sat up. "Luke?"

By concentrating and pushing past the pain, he was able to mumble, "Sleep," and squeeze her hand with what he desperately hoped was reassurance.

When he ought to be whispering sweet words of

love and holding her close, all he could do was lie there. He couldn't feel anything, couldn't hear her breathing, even though she was very close, couldn't see to the end of the bed, couldn't smell the lavender in her hair, even though a stray tendril brushed his nose.

Drowsy, clearly sated, she curled up next to him and lazily rubbed her head against his chest. "Yeah, I'm really tired, too," she said with a yawn. "We'll talk more in the morning."

The morning. Luke's only hope was that a few hours of sleep would restore his fried circuits, reknit his synapses, soothe his shattered nerves.

He was not a praying man, but he didn't have any other choice.

Please, God, let me be okay in the morning. At least long enough to talk to Gilly.

His body craved sleep, surfeit, rest, and he had no choice but to give in. He closed his eyes. Morning. He would wait until morning to assess the damage.

WHEN SHE AWOKE, Luke was still asleep, with the black sheet tangled around his waist. He lay on his side, breathing deeply, his lashes dark and thick against his cheek.

God, he was gorgeous. A lazy smile drifted over her lips. If she'd ever worried about his health, she had no fear now. Last night had proved, once and for all, that Luke was in tip-top shape. Tip-top. Her smile widened.

When Luke woke up, she'd tell him again how much she loved him, how good they were together.

"He said he loves me, too," she whispered. "Okay, maybe he shouldn't be held to heat-of-the-moment words in the light of day. But he'll say it again. Lots and lots.''

At the moment, however, she had other concerns. Like the fact that she was stark naked, her stomach was growling, and Luke looked like he might be sacked out for hours.

She chuckled. ''Had a hard night, poor baby.''

First thing on the agenda was to find something to wear, because the scraps of Suzette's dress were not going to be much help. She marched to Luke's closet. He had several white dress shirts hanging there, so she took one, buttoning it down to her knees.

But not much else would do. ''Hmm,'' she mused, eyeing the back of the closet. There was that nifty secret passageway that led to a whole roomful of old clothes. Maybe she could find a pair of pants or a skirt. Besides, she always had been curious about that secret room. So she slid back the false back, scooted through the passage and came upon the storage room, just like she remembered.

It was a great place, full of trunks and boxes, and she wandered a bit, finding some lace knickers and a pair of thick socks, an old pair of blue jeans that fit rather nicely, and a straw hat she would've liked to take home for a summer garden party.

As she continued to poke, she paused. How funny. There was a trunk of old sporting equipment, with jerseys and padded hockey pants lying around as if they'd just been used. Who would be using out-of-date hockey uniforms in this household?

But she dismissed it from her mind, spying a coat-rack in the corner and remembering it immediately. It was the one that always used to be in the front hall. Now, relegated to the secret closet, it held a huge old raccoon coat that looked promising, at least to get her home in. She donned it, feeling very Roaring Twenties, and paused long enough to note the other things on the rack—a big black trench coat and a brown one, too, as well as several old-fashioned hats. Humphrey Bogart hats, she thought, twirling one around her finger.

Humphrey Bogart hats?

She stopped. She reached for the only other items hanging there, old cashmere scarves. She held one of them, brushing its softness between her fingers, remembering exactly what it had felt like to sink her hands inside Nightshade's scarf when she'd touched his face.

Nightshade.

The hats. The coats. The scarves. The bottom dropped out of her stomach.

She supposed if she went snooping around long enough, she would find various pairs of sunglasses and gloves, too.

Luke was Nightshade. One and the same.

Chapter Fourteen

She stood there clutching the scarf, as her mind reeled.

But Luke *couldn't* be Nightshade. Nightshade was bigger, broader, taller.

Okay, so maybe a coat, hat and padding had made him seem bigger.

But it was impossible! Luke wouldn't leave the house, and Nightshade was running around saving people. Besides, hadn't she been talking to Luke on the phone at school while Nightshade was still disappearing down the hall?

Not even Luke could be two places at once.

And then again, after Nightshade had paid his late-night visit, slipping in and out through the window, she'd called Luke not five minutes later. He couldn't have had time to climb down the fire escape, walk to his car, race home, and get to the phone!

Except that Aunt Abby had stalled. And Luke was breathless when he finally spoke to her.

She sat down on a trunk with a thump.

It all fit. Luke's lifelong friendship—Nightshade's "emotional ties" to West Riverside. Luke's tender ribs—Nightshade's padding. Luke's dark shadowy house—Nightshade in sunglasses. Luke's sensitive hearing—Nightshade whispering, "Just know that when you're in trouble, I will hear you."

And the worst of all, Nightshade's mind-numbing kisses matched up with Luke's dazzling embrace. One and the same.

"How could I have been such an idiot?" she demanded. She'd even had a dream about Nightshade and woken up murmuring Luke's name! Her subconscious knew all along even if her conscious mind was sticking its head in the sand.

The word "fool" might as well have been etched on her forehead.

Furious with him, furious with herself, she snatched a scarf and one of the fedoras from the coatrack, scrambling for the passage and the closet back into Luke's room.

He was still in bed, damn him. Not for long.

She whipped the scarf at him, and when he didn't wake up, pitched the fedora like that guy in the James Bond movies.

"Wake up," she demanded.

But still he slept on.

She crossed her arms over the ridiculous raccoon coat. At least it covered the rest of her outfit. It should've been hard to be mean and angry when you were dressed like a refugee from "The Munsters." But she wasn't having any trouble.

All she had to do was think of Nightshade and the damn bedroom-window escapade that made her feel guilty for cheating on Luke, and her fury rose higher than ever. She'd been manipulated. Used. Made a fool of.

Still, Luke slept like a baby, not even noticing the furious woman standing there and staring a hole in him. She frowned. Was it possible he was playing possum to avoid her attack of temper? That was even lower than pretending to be Nightshade and making a monkey out of her all this time.

Suddenly the images of kisses and lovemaking, of Nightshade's disguise and Luke's lies all rolled together, and she felt completely overwhelmed. She just couldn't deal with it anymore. If he wanted to pretend to be asleep, so be it. A haze of anger and love and betrayal clouded her vision, and she knew she had to get out of there before she strangled him.

Picking up the remains of her dress, her heels, and the keys to the Ferrari from the floor, Gilly ran for the door. As she cleared the doorway, she thought she heard a sound from the bed, and she whirled around.

"Did you say something?" she asked.

His eyes remained closed, and he didn't respond. Gilly chewed her lip. His behavior was so weird she felt a faint ripple of alarm, as if maybe something was wrong. Luke had been ill before, or at least put on a good show of it. Was it possible that making love had put him over the top somehow?

She didn't waver for long.

"No," she told herself forcefully. "Whatever his story is, I'm not buying it. He's obviously breathing, and that's more than he deserves at the moment."

She roared back down to her apartment in his jazzy car, dumping it right out in front in a No Parking zone and sprinting up the steps in her stocking feet. She had barely opened her apartment door when Mrs. Mooshman came running up, resplendent in her lime green running suit, complete with NOD Squad cap, flashlight and a brand-new whistle.

"Oh, Gilly, honey! What a relief!" Her neighbor

squeezed her for all she was worth. Then she squinted at Gilly. "What are you wearing?" She added, "We were so worried."

"Why?" Gilly detached herself enough to see Mr. Zamechnik, Suzette and Tony Fielder and his mother crowding into the third-floor hall. "What is this?"

"It's an emergency meeting of OGW," Mr. Zamechnik explained, elbowing his way in front of Mrs. Mooshman and stopping the woman in midbreath. That earned him a dirty look, but he forged right on. "The school principal, Mrs. Sheffield, and young Tony were on duty last night at the Snow Ball, but circumstances being what they were, they lost you."

Gilly glanced from face to face. "OGW? I thought it was the NOD Squad."

"No, no, that's different," Mrs. M said, squeezing back around the old man. "That's Neighborhood Observers and Defenders. This is Operation Gillian Watch."

As if she hadn't had enough humiliation for one day, Gilly thought. Now it seemed she was at the center of some damn watch. "What is this? You've all been *spying* on me?"

"No, of course not," Suzette hastened to assure her. "After that newspaper article where you said you were going to put yourself in danger on purpose, we were very concerned about you. So your aunt and uncle formed a little committee to keep an eye on you."

"My aunt and uncle? I know where that came from," she said darkly. "Luke."

"No, no, it came directly from your aunt and uncle." Mrs. Mooshman's round eyes were guileless. "And that's why—I'm sure you'll understand the thinking here—we had to call the Fitzhughs and let them know when you were still missing this morning.''

"But I wasn't missing! I was—" She broke off. "Somewhere that is none of your business."

"With Lucas Blackthorn, right?" Suzette asked with a smile. "The two of you were looking pretty cozy last night." She shrugged sheepishly. "I tried to tell them you were probably with him."

"No, no," Tony interjected. "She was with that cool Nightshade guy. That's your boyfriend, right?"

"You mean you haven't heard?" Mr. Zamechnik said.

Everybody turned his way.

"What could he know?" Mrs. Mooshman scowled. "Be quiet, old man, and stop wasting our time."

But Suzette was the first to voice the question everyone else was thinking. "Heard what?"

"Why, that Mr. Blackthorn and Mr. Nightshade are the same person. I mean, Lucas Blackthorn *is* Nightshade. Or Nightshade is Luke Blackthorn. Something like that." Mr. Z raised his hands in confusion. "That Devon Drake broke the story last night. I saw it in the paper this morning and heard it on the radio, also. The Drake woman said she had witnesses who saw Nightshade round up some ruffians at the Snow Ball, and then he went and stuffed his coat and hat in the trunk of his car, and presto—he turned back into Lucas Blackthorn!''

"The Ferrari," Gilly groaned. "The trunk was open! So he'd just dumped his disguise in there. Oh, God, I am even stupider than I thought." No doubt, clothes similar to those she'd found in the secret room were still in his trunk.

"You mean you knew?" Suzette squealed.

"You mean you didn't know?" Mrs. Mooshman shrieked.

"I didn't know. Until this morning." Gilly turned to Mr. Zamechnik. "Can I see that paper?"

It didn't take her long to scan the story or to realize Luke was in danger. "They said they would make him pay, and he's up there all by himself," she whispered.

"You can't be serious. Not after this!" Suzette took one of Gilly's arms, while Tony Fielder's mother came up on the other side.

"Ms. Quinn, you don't want to feel sorry for him. Why, he lied to you, pretending to be this Nightshade character." Mrs. Fielder's deep brown eyes were lit with concern. "You take it from me, Ms. Quinn. You don't need no double-dealing scum of a man. You do fine all by yourself."

"Oh, no, I'm not forgiving him," Gilly asserted. "I'm still really mad at him. But he could be in trouble, what with the mayor and his thugs on the loose, and Luke pinpointed as Nightshade, and Uncle Fitz and Aunt Abby out of town."

"The mayor and his thugs?" Suzette echoed.

"Oh, yes." She'd almost forgotten about that part. But the sooner she announced the truth, the sooner West Riverside would be out of danger. "The mayor and that Ed Spivak from the Lucky Lady casinos have been behind all these muggings and robberies. The alley, the burglary at your place, Mrs. M, the punk who came in my window and all those thieves last night at the Snow Ball—they paid them to do it."

"No!" Suzette exclaimed, her eyes round.

"Yes," Gilly said. "We have proof. Luke overheard a very damaging conversation."

The same thing occurred to them all at the same

time. "Then he really may be in danger," Suzette concluded. Tony and Mr. Zamechnik nodded gravely.

Gilly shivered, remembering that evil sneering voice in her bedroom. *Tell your boyfriend Nightshade... sunglasses ain't no shield against bullets.*

"But the Fitzhughs ought to be back any time," Mrs. Mooshman put in. "I called them at about five this morning to report you were missing, and they started right home. So at least he won't be alone."

"But he was when I left." Gilly chewed her lip. She was beginning to get a very bad feeling about all this. "It could take them hours to get home." All she could think of was Luke lying in that bed, hardly moving, not waking up even when she'd thrown a hat at him.

The ripple of alarm expanded into a roller coaster.

"Call him," she ordered Mrs. Mooshman, pushing the woman in the direction of her apartment. But instead, Mrs. M flipped open a cellular phone and handed it to Gilly, who punched in the number as fast as she could. "No answer." She looked around wildly. "I have to go back up there. I can't leave him by himself."

"You can't go alone," Suzette argued. "We'll all go."

"But we won't all fit in the Ferrari, and I don't have any other car!"

"Mr. Zamechnik's car," Mrs. Mooshman started. "That big old wreck is plenty big for six. Come on, everyone. Time's a-wastin'!" She blew her whistle as if to start a race. "Let's get a move on, people!"

And so they all ran downstairs and piled into Mr. Zamechnik's ancient smoke-belching Ford, with Mr. Z driving at a snail's pace and Mrs. M ordering him to go faster and to take a different route. Tony laughed out loud, enjoying the adventure, while Suzette and Mrs. Fielder compared notes on the perfidy of men and plotted how to expose the crooked mayor. Gilly bit her nails, praying they got to Luke in time.

Because no matter how angry she was at him, no matter how hurt her feelings were, one thing remained. She still loved him. She loved him desperately, passionately, with all her heart and soul. He had to be okay. He just had to. She needed a chance to punish him, to forgive him, to make up.

And if he was hurt or injured, she would kill whoever did it. With her bare hands.

Right after she killed Luke for causing her so much worry.

HE HAD TRIED to call out to her. But his powers of speech were still not working. All he managed was some kind of damn little whimper that made him sound more like a mouse than a man.

Rage filled him. Because lying there, as lifelike as a hunk of salami, he'd known it was all over. Happiness had been here one moment and gone the next.

The hat on the bed told the tale.

Gilly had found one of Nightshade's fedoras. And she was furious.

Even if he had wanted to wallow in his morning-after misery, he didn't have time. He had no sooner taken inventory of his various body parts to find out what was working and what wasn't when he heard the noise downstairs.

"Gilly?" he called out, his voice sounding like a rusty hinge.

"I heard him," a man yelled. "Upstairs."

And that was when Luke realized the second great truth of the morning. *His powers were gone.* It sounded as if a gang of not very polite thugs had just invaded his home, and he hadn't even noticed until it was too late. Luke could hear them as they neared, just the way anybody else would, but nothing more. He couldn't smell them, he couldn't feel the pounding of their footfalls, and the light from the open window wasn't doing a thing.

His powers were gone.

"Check the room down the hall," a different voice called out. "I looked at the ones on this side. Hey, Little Boy Nightshade, where are you?"

"We gonna get you, wherever you hiding," the first thug said in a singsong voice. He sounded familiar, like the guy from the alley maybe. "Hey, man, I like that picture in the hallway. Remind me to take that with me after I beat the crap out of pretty boy."

Luke almost laughed aloud. There were thugs in his house, threatening to beat the tar out of him, and he was euphoric.

Because he could see, he could hear, he could smell—just like anybody else.

But the gang of miscreants was getting closer, and he knew he had to put some kind of plan together. Because there was no way in hell he was going to lie there like a Christmas turkey and get beaten to a bloody pulp. Unfortunately, he had very few weapons at his disposal.

He tensed, gathering the sheet around him, wishing he at least was wearing pants. Every movement was stiff and strange, every muscle ached, and he knew this wasn't going to be easy. No outrunning, no overpowering. All he had were his wits.

Well, he'd been here before, hadn't he?

Wearing the sheet, he rolled clumsily off the bed and closed his hand over the only thing on the dresser. A camera, of course.

He had no time to think about strategy as the thugs came thundering down the hall. Dropping his sheet in front of the door, Luke slid behind the thick drapes at the window, close enough to see the intruders clearly, but hidden from their view. The first one had a dirty bandanna tied around his head, and he stood in the doorway, squinting into the dim room. "Where are you, pretty boy? You wouldn't hide from me, now would you?"

He got pushed aside when the other two—a tall, skinny guy with a bright yellow Mohawk and a big bruiser with bulging muscles—got stuck in the door together, each unwilling to let the other pass.

Great. Other people got cold efficient gangsters who broke in, got the job done and took off. Luke got the Three Stooges.

"Jeez, you guys can't even come in a door right." The leader of this grimy little band, the small one in the bandanna, motioned for the big lug to block the doorway. "Where are you, Nightshade?" He padded softly into the room. "Hiding under the bed or something? We know you're in here. Come out nice and slow. We ain't gonna hurt you. We just wanna play is all."

Luke seized the moment. It might not be perfect, but he couldn't bet on getting a better one. Hopping out from behind the door, he focused his camera on the small guy, hitting the flash attachment and blinding him momentarily, and then he tossed the camera itself at Mohawk Man's head.

It connected with a satisfying *thump*. The big guy stayed in the doorway, looking wary. Luke dropped to his knees and jerked on the bedsheet, pulling the mountain of a man off his feet and on top of the other two.

They would recover quickly, but by then, Luke planned to be safely ensconced in the secret passageway. As he pushed his aching muscles into a heroic leap over the top of the thugs, Luke just wished he'd had time to get some pants.

THERE WERE no other cars in the driveway, and the house seemed quiet and dark.

"Uncle Fitz? Aunt Abby?" Gilly whispered. "Is anyone here?"

Stomp. Clunk.

Someone was definitely there. And she had never heard Luke make that much noise in her life.

"Hey, man, there's all kinds of good stuff in this place," a rough voice called from upstairs. "You should see this cool TV. And tons of camera stuff we could get some money for. I think we should forget about pretty boy and take the loot. He ain't coming back, man."

"He's here somewhere. Keep lookin'!" a more menacing voice yelled back.

"Man, this place is deserted. He ain't here."

"Keep lookin'!"

Gilly put her finger to her lips to signal everyone for silence, as they all tiptoed in.

"Be careful!" she whispered. "Tony, you and your mother stay here by the door. You're our lookout."

"I'll go this way!" Mr. Zamechnik announced, sneaking off to the back before Gilly had a chance to catch him.

"You moron!" Mrs. Mooshman said, running after him.

Gilly just watched them go, any hope of organizing this rescue party spinning down the drain.

"You find Luke," Suzette whispered. She grabbed a candlestick and hid behind the banister. "If anyone comes this way, I'll brain 'em!"

"Okay. I guess." Gilly began to creep up the stairs, but she stopped in midstep when the very audible sound of the garage door opening echoed throughout the house. Aunt Abby and Uncle Fitz. And not a moment too soon.

"What was that?" the voice from upstairs demanded.

"Man, I don't know."

"Cops? Let's blow."

Suddenly the sharp hiss of a whistle pierced the air. "You stop right there!" Mrs. Mooshman's unmistakable voice cried. "I see you, you pervert!"

There was the sound of running feet from one room to the next. Gilly raced up the steps in time to see Mrs. Mooshman blowing her whistle in the face of a very thin, black-leather-clad man with a bright yellow Mohawk. He looked scared to death. Or maybe he was in pain from the whistle blasting so close to his ear.

"Stop that, you old bag!" He reached out to grab her just as Mr. Zamechnik tapped him on the shoulder from behind. The punk whirled, and Mr. Z sprayed a canister of mace in his face.

"From the NOD Squad," the old man said modestly.

"Nicely done," Gilly said admiringly.

"We'll tie him up and dump him in the front hall. But there're at least two more," Mrs. Mooshman announced, taking a moment to breathe. "Be careful."

"You, too." But somehow Gilly was sure Mr. Z and Mrs. M would be just fine.

She raced for Luke's room. He wasn't there. It was eerily quiet, considering the place had been totally trashed. The mattress had been half dragged off the bed, the curtains pulled down and piled in a heap, and the sensory-deprivation tank knocked off its pedestal and leaking a steady stream of water. One of Luke's black bedsheets had been ripped to pieces.

"Oh, my God! Luke? Luke?" Where could he be?

And then she heard the knock coming from the back of the closet. "Gilly?" a strange, raspy voice called. "Is that you? The door is stuck from this side. Open it, will you?"

Gilly leaped over to the closet, grabbed open the secret panel and darted in, almost tripping over Luke. He was naked and a little wobbly, and he had what looked like a whopper of a black eye, but he looked gorgeous to her.

"Oh, God, Luke." She pulled him into her arms and hugged the stuffing out of him. And then she caught herself and backed off quickly. "Are you okay? What happened to your eye? Did those animals do that? Did they do something to your voice, too?"

"Gilly, um, could we…talk about this later?" he managed. "I need pants."

"You need pants?" She almost wept with relief, kissing him all over his face, careful to avoid his swollen, bruised eye. But as she kissed him, he slid down the wall, ending up in a sitting position. "Oh, I'm sorry! Does it hurt badly? Oh, God, Luke, they could've killed you!''

But he shook his head. "I'm fine, Gilly. I got the black eye by accident. I ran into a door in the secret passage. It was dark. My powers are gone," he said bluntly. "Otherwise I'm just very tired. Aftereffects, I think. But no more bionic boy. No more freak.''

"I haven't got a clue what you're talking about, but I'm sure we can sort this out later." She joined him on the floor and hugged him again. "Bionic boy? Is that something to do with the Nightshade thing?''

"Uh-huh." He leaned against her, taking a deep breath, and she could hear that his voice was already getting better. "I'm moving a little slowly now, but I think I'm going to be fine. You don't know what a relief this is—I can hear and see and smell, just like anyone. The eye—it's painful, but just like anyone else would feel. And I can make love to you, Gilly, any time I want.''

His hands clasped her behind the head as he tried to maneuver her over for a kiss.

"Now is not a good time," she said with a laugh. "I thought all you wanted was some pants.''

"I'm willing to negotiate.''

"But you do some of your best work without pants.''

He dipped her back onto the floor, pressing closer. "I know.''

So she kissed him back, ignoring for the moment that he was naked, that he had a black eye, that they were in a secret passage, that there was a battle royal going on in the house around them. "I love you, Luke. If anything had happened to you...''

His eyes become more serious. "I love you, too, Gilly. Always."

Her heart warmed, brimmed over. Okay, so she was still a little miffed at all the deception and subterfuge. And someday she would make him pay for that midnight visit when he haunted her dreams and stoked her desire and then left her flat. But right now she had better things to do.

After just a few kisses, they both knew this would have to wait. He found some clothes, and then the two of them ventured out to check on the rest of the gang.

As they hit the second-floor landing, a commotion exploded below them. Gilly stopped, leaning over to watch, as a huge man pounded into the hall, coming right up in front of the newel, where Suzette popped up and bonked him with her candlestick. As he wavered, staring stupidly, Uncle Fitz stomped in from the other direction and punched him in the gut, and Tony leaped onto his back, grabbing his hair and screaming in his ear.

The man lurched this way and that, finally dropping to his knees with a thunderous roar. As Tony hopped off, the big thug toppled over onto his face, right next to the bound-and-gagged Mohawk guy, who had apparently been left there by Mrs. Mooshman.

Then Tony, Suzette and Uncle Fitz exchanged high fives.

"Come back here!" yelled Aunt Abby from the direction of the kitchen.

Everybody else stood and watched as a smaller man wearing a bandanna barreled down the hallway with Abby in hot pursuit. The little creep saw the crowd ahead of him, stopped in his tracks, and Aunt Abigail caught up.

"Take that!" she cried, giving him a roundhouse blow with her frying pan.

Down he went, spinning and tumbling right on top of his comrades, all in a neat pile.

And that, as they say, was that.

Well, not quite. Just as the frying pan found its mark, Devon Drake stuck her head in the front door. "Gillian Quinn? Are you here?"

Gilly waved her hand weakly from the second-floor landing.

"Ms. Quinn, this very nice lady outside, a Mrs. Fielder, has been telling me that this whole attack was set up by the mayor. Is that true?"

"Yes, it is." Still a little unsteady, but on his feet and looking mighty fine, Luke put his arm around Gilly. "All because of the casino project."

Aunt Abigail shrieked when she saw his eye, Uncle Fitz came racing up the stairs, and Gilly braced herself.

But Luke waved them away. "We can fill you in on the details later," he said coolly. "Right now, I need to go to bed for about twelve hours." He paused. He sent Gilly a mischievous smile. "Gilly? Coming with me?"

Suzette, Mrs. Fielder and Uncle Fitz laughed, Mrs. Mooshman put her hands over Tony's ears, Aunt Abby gulped, the pile of burglars moaned, Devon Drake scribbled in her notebook, and Gilly blushed down to her toes.

But she lifted her chin and met Luke's blue blue gaze. "I think my place is a better idea. Yours is kind of a mess," she said sweetly. "Are you game for a ride in Mr. Zamechnik's Ford?"

"Why don't we take the limo?" He brushed her cheek with his lips. "Fitz can drive."

Gilly just smiled.

"But, Ms. Quinn—what about the mayor? What about my story?" cried Devon Drake.

"It can wait." Gilly looped her arm through Luke's and guided him down the steps as Devon continued to protest. "It can wait," Gilly said more firmly. "After all, I have my priorities."

And she and the mysterious Nightshade walked out the front door into a bright white winter morning.

EVER HAD ONE OF THOSE DAYS?

TO DO:

☑ at the supermarket buying two dozen muffins that your son just remembered to tell you he needed for the school treat, you realize you left your wallet at home

☑ at work just as you're going into the big meeting, you discover your son took your presentation to school, and you have his hand-drawn superhero comic book

☑ your mother-in-law calls to say she's coming for a month-long visit

☑ finally at the end of a long and exasperating day, you escape from it all with an entertaining, humorous and always romantic Love & Laughter book!

ENJOY
LOVE & LAUGHTER™
EVERY DAY!

For a preview, turn the page....

Here's a sneak peek at
Carrie Alexander's THE AMOROUS HEIRESS
Available September 1997...

————————

"YOU'RE A VERY popular lady," Jed Kelley observed as Augustina closed the door on her suitors.

She waved a hand. "Just two of a dozen." Technically true since her grandmother had put her on the open market. "You're not afraid of a little competition, are you?"

"Competition?" He looked puzzled. "I thought the position was mine."

Augustina shook her head, smiling coyly. "You didn't think Grandmother was the final arbiter of the decision, did you? I say a trial period is in order." No matter that Jed Kelley had miraculously passed Grandmother's muster, Augustina felt the need for a little propriety. But, on the other hand, she could be married before the summer was out and be free as a bird, with the added bonus of a husband it wouldn't be all that difficult to learn to love.

She got up the courage to reach for his hand, and then just like that, she—Miss Gussy Gutless Fairchild—was holding Jed Kelley's hand. He looked down at their linked hands. "Of course, you don't really know what sort of work I can do, do you?"

A funny way to put it, she thought absently, cradling his callused hand between both of her own. "We can get to know each other, and then, if that works out..." she murmured. *Wow.* If she'd known what this arranged marriage thing was all about, she'd have been a supporter of Grandmother's campaign from the start!

"Are you a palm reader?" Jed asked gruffly. His voice was as raspy as sandpaper and it was rubbing her all the right ways, but the question flustered her. She dropped his hand.

"I'm sorry."

"No problem," he said, "as long as I'm hired."

"Hired!" she scoffed. "What a way of putting it!"

Jed folded his arms across his chest. "So we're back to the trial period."

"Yes." Augustina frowned and her gaze dropped to his work boots. Okay, so he wasn't as well off as the majority of her suitors, but really, did he think she was going to *pay* him to marry her?

"Fine, then." He flipped her a wave and, speechless, she watched him leave. She was trembling all over like a malaria victim in a snowstorm, shot with hot charges and cold shivers until her brain was numb. This couldn't be true. Fantasy men didn't happen to nice girls like her.

"Augustina?"

Her grandmother's voice intruded on Gussy's privacy. "Ahh. There you are. I see you met the new gardener?"

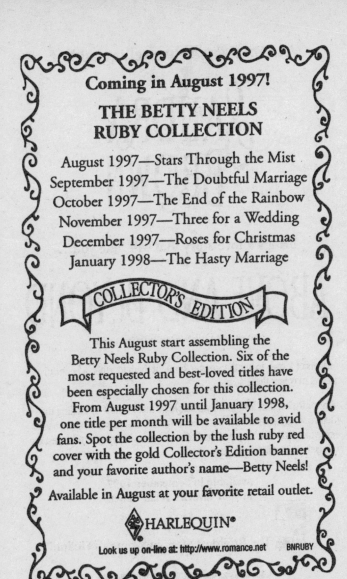

Coming in August 1997!

THE BETTY NEELS RUBY COLLECTION

August 1997—Stars Through the Mist
September 1997—The Doubtful Marriage
October 1997—The End of the Rainbow
November 1997—Three for a Wedding
December 1997—Roses for Christmas
January 1998—The Hasty Marriage

COLLECTOR'S EDITION

This August start assembling the
Betty Neels Ruby Collection. Six of the
most requested and best-loved titles have
been especially chosen for this collection.
From August 1997 until January 1998,
one title per month will be available to avid
fans. Spot the collection by the lush ruby red
cover with the gold Collector's Edition banner
and your favorite author's name—Betty Neels!

Available in August at your favorite retail outlet.

◆ HARLEQUIN®

HARLEQUIN®
A M E R I C A N ◆ R O M A N C E ®

You loved the original "How To Marry..." trilogy so much that we're bringing you more of the fun and excitement of husband-hunting!

Join Pam McCutcheon in September 1997 for those all-important pointers on how to catch that reluctant—but oh-so-sexy—rogue!

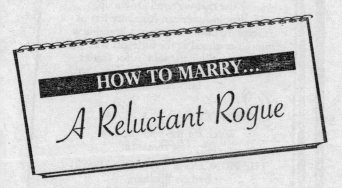

HOW TO MARRY...

A Reluctant Rogue

Don't miss
How To Marry...
A RELUCTANT ROGUE (#696)
September 1997

And watch for more "How To Marry..." titles coming in the months ahead!

Available wherever Harlequin books are sold.